MY JOURNEY TO RECOVERY

SOBER

JESSICA
WHALEN

innovo PUBLISHING

Published by Innovo Publishing, LLC
www.innovopublishing.com
1-888-546-2111

Providing Full-Service Publishing Services for Christian Authors, Artists
& Ministries: Hardbacks, Paperbacks, eBooks, Audiobooks, Music,
Screenplays, & Courses

SOBER
My Journey to Recovery

ISBN: 978-1-61314-578-4

Cover Design & Interior Layout: Innovo Publishing, LLC

Printed in the United States of America
U.S. Printing History
First Edition: 2020

Dedication

To everyone who loved me when I could not love myself.

Contents

MY JOURNEY TO RECOVERY

SOBER

PART I

SEARCHING THE DEPTHS

Day 1

Pacing back and forth. Front to back. Side to side. *My God! Help me! What am I to do?*

I just got home from a therapy session, and my therapist, X,[1] was pretty upset about my latest binge drinking episode. She told me, "Something needs to change because what we are doing isn't working. You need something more." My reaction was a mix of, "Well, obviously!" and, "Let's give what we're doing some more time," and, "Screw you!" I did not know what I needed. I didn't even know what I wanted. I only knew that I was hurting and that I was hurting those around me. *Decisions. Decisions.*

I stopped pacing and sat down. I looked up Alcoholics Anonymous® online and took a quiz assessing my drinking behavior. It was twenty questions, and it told me if I answered "yes" to three or more of them then I was "definitely" an alcoholic.

I answered "yes" to eleven of them. The clues about what I should do were building up.

When I was in grad school, I took a class on substance abuse. One assignment was for me to attend two local Alcoholics Anonymous meetings. It was a cool assignment at the time. Little did I know back then that that assignment planted a seed that would bloom four years later.

In that class, the professor shared with everyone on the last day that he was in recovery himself from alcohol. It was an inspiring testimony. He had come to mind when I was pacing back and forth. I knew if I had a drinking problem, I should look for help in the rooms I had entered years before.

That night, I went to an A.A. meeting for the first time, and I picked up a white chip. That day was the first day of this wild ride of sobriety. I am miserable. But I feel hope for the first time in a long time. I am sober. Period.

~1 day sober

---

1. Pseudonym.

Hope

"It's not that I wanted the help so much at the time; I simply did not want to hurt like that again." —Quote from *Daily Reflections*[2]

I'm so tired of hurting and then healing, hurting and then healing. Whenever I heal, I'm making progress on some issues but not on the most devastating issue of them all: my self-hatred, self-rejection, and self-destruction. I fool everyone . . . at times, even myself.

At the core of it all, I have a fervent desire to kill myself. Since my faith deters me from suicide, I set out to make myself feel like the worthless person that I believe I am. Interestingly, through my faith, I believe my body to be a temple. Yet I do little to uphold my end of the bargain of protecting it and treating it with respect. My scars, my heartburn, my shaky hands, and my fluctuating weight are dead giveaways of my lack of self-respect. My self-destruction affects more than just me, and this further adds to my guilt and self-hatred.

I can no longer drown in my sorrows. I cannot drink away my pain into temporary non-existence. I will still hurt, but not in the same self-loathing cycle. I have hope now. I don't have to hurt myself like that anymore. I feel a warmth inside my chest. I feel I'm finally accessing the broken adolescent inside of me. It's time to work through everything and finally heal—and, of course, maintain.

~3 days sober

Personal Reflections

Sobriety is exhausting. Relentless thoughts! Relentless desires! Both of the freedoms of sobriety and the "freedoms" of drinking. I am on vacation with my mom. Such a wicked time to try to get sober! I was so convinced of Mom's betrayal. I tried to believe she was drinking behind my back after saying she would not. Of course she wasn't. I was being paranoid. Was it my fear of not being accepted with this latest fold in my identity? Was it me hoping there would be a "valid reason" to drink again? I'm only 5 days sober; what's the harm in drinking again . . . just one more time?

---

2. *Daily Reflections* (2016), p. 24.

But this thinking leads to death. That's what I'm told, and that is what I was reminded of when I reached out to a member of A.A. for help. This disease progresses whether I consume alcohol or not.

Life. Or. Death.

~5 days sober

One week sober. I've made it this far. I feel more hopeful now that I can make it further. It was only two days ago when I wasn't sure if I could make it through the next hour sober, let alone the next two days! I was telling myself two days ago that there wasn't a big difference between January 13th and January 18th, but I'm grateful God helped me find strength to stay away from the drink because today I feel wonderful being 7 days sober!

One day at a time. *God, please, continue to grant me serenity to accept the things I cannot change, the courage to change the things that I can, and the wisdom to know the difference. For you are the Way, the Truth, and the Life. Amen.*

~7 days sober

Sobriety freaking sucks. Focusing on the next time I *could* drink was incredibly less stressful than focusing on (in addition to coping with and distracting from) *not* drinking. I feel tired, bored, and depressed. I don't want to go to a meeting, but I know I need to.

~9 days sober

Relapse Reflection

I'm told I don't have to feel defeated because I'm an alcoholic. It is something I'm powerless over. No human power can cure me from my alcoholism. This is not to say I don't have power over my decisions. It is just to say I don't have to feel like crap for being a hypocrite between the message I preach in my day job as a counselor and the actions I take with alcohol at night. Because, after all, I'm a freakin' alcoholic.

~1 day sober

Dear Alcohol: Part I

Dear Alcohol,

Screw you.

You slowly became the most important thing in my life. You slowly fed me lies that I believed to be truths. You told me you would never hurt me. You told me you would protect me. You told me you would make me feel better.

I sit here now, on the cusp of my twenty-eighth birthday, broke, overweight, in pain, betrayed, and heartbroken by you. Betrayal is a major source of my pain and a trigger for me. You know this. You comforted me innumerable times as I worked to heal my wounds from past betrayals. But this whole time, you were betraying me, and I didn't even know it.

Slowly, our relationship progressed from a glass of wine to a full bottle of wine at night. Slowly, our relationship escalated from engaging two nights a week to engaging seven nights a week. Before I knew it, we engaged almost every day or night, or both, for an entire year.

Oh, the lies! You lied! You are a liar. You told me if I just had a glass of you then I would fall asleep quickly and sleep soundly. Here is a primary example of your deceit. You knew I valued my independence, but you kept whispering to me how simple it would be to just have a glass of you and all my sleep struggles would suddenly stop. I listened to your solution of depending on you. I anticipated this to be a temporary solution. Little did I realize at the time, a year and a half ago, that you were manipulating me. Because work, it did! Sleep soundly, I did! So, if one glass of you worked, two glasses must work even better! And then your taste . . . so satisfying and liberating that it felt like I was quenching a thirst of my soul. Then I thought, *If I start drinking you early enough, I can drink even more than two glasses, sleep soundly, and still go to work the next morning just fine.*

Well, that didn't work out too well. When I came home after work feeling hungover and awful from our time the night before, I would pour myself another glass of you to feel better. As I said, you weren't quenching a thirst on a biological/survival level, you were quenching a thirst on a deeper level. You were restorative. I see now you were restoring me from the destruction you caused. It was a vicious cycle.

For all the allegiance I pledged you, you certainly were mean to me. It got to the point where I had only a sip of vodka and then I had bad heartburn for the next several days. In those times I would switch to white wine for a while. You messed with my body temperature, causing irregularities throughout the day and night. I would be in session with a client, and I would randomly start sweating, or my face would turn red without an actual cause or reasoning behind it. I would have night sweats—sometimes to the point of having to get up and change clothes.

Towards the end of our time together, my hands began shaking when I wasn't consuming you. This concerned me. I brought this concern to you, and you offered a solution. As soon as I drank you again, you made it go away. My weight went up and down. When I used you and when you used me, I ate so I didn't throw you up. The more I engaged with you, the less I worked out. The more time I spent with you, the less time I spent taking care of myself.

In my fight for survival, I clung to you. Little did I know you were killing me.

~5 days sober

Insanity vs. Sanity

What is my definition of insanity?

- Instability
- Self-harm
- Self-destruction
- Doubt
- Obsession
- Impulsivity
- Artificial feelings (alcohol-numbing/feeling nothing)
- Avoiding/running from the truth
- Asking, "Why?"
- Quitting, starting, quitting, starting, quitting, starting
- Irrationality
- Irresponsibility
- Suicidality
- Isolation
- Brokenness
- Failed attempts to succeed

What is my definition of sanity? What does God want me to be like?
- Love; loving Him, loving myself, loving others
- Forgiveness; forgiving myself, forgiving others
- Light
- Hope
- Safety
- Wholeness
- All-consuming, overflowing love
- Emotion
- Fullness
- Acceptance
- Clear mind

~9 days sober

Hi, My Name is Jessica, and I'm an Alcoholic

H *i, my name is Jessica, and I'm an alcoholic.*

That sentence becomes easier to say every day, but the struggle of being in early recovery does not. I have moments where I both feel and think I know a little of what it means to be a "grateful alcoholic." Other times, I can barely fathom ending my day any other way than with alcohol. However, my sponsor, P.[3] speaks truth I cannot unhear. I've attended meetings I can never un-attend. I've read facts I can never unread.

Right now, it *feels* like I'm limiting my life, but I *know* I'm expanding it. I'm becoming reacquainted with myself. I went to the gym two days in a row this week. On day two, I texted P. I did so to document that I'm following through with her suggestions, to celebrate said following through, and to build accountability. She responded, "Sober life rocks." Maybe it was the expectation of a different response, or maybe it was because I truly understood P's statement! Outside of being with my three-year-old niece, Blakely, I smiled bigger and more genuinely than I had in a long, long time.

It was then that I realized that for the past one-and-a-half years of my life, I would have been home already drinking . . . not at the gym. From ages sixteen to twenty-six (plus or minus some periods of time), I always found time for the gym. The gym is and always has been my

---

3. Pseudonym.

greatest antidepressant, my greatest therapist. As I described in my definition of insanity, my pattern of the past one-and-a-half (plus) years has been to start, stop, start over, etcetera, etcetera, etcetera. In that time, the feelings of hopelessness and utter defeat became ever so familiar. Coincidentally (I think not!), so did my alcohol use.

As I'm writing this, I'm realizing how the start, stop, start over cycle and associated feelings of defeat and hopelessness parallels early sobriety. I'm starting the mornings strong, and I'm finishing the days weak, tired, and craving alcohol. Feeling defeated. Feeling triggered. Not necessarily by the exhaustion but perhaps by the expectations that this day truly was going to be easier than the last. And, one day it will be . . . is what I'm told . . . but then the last three days in a row weren't by the end of the night. They sucked. I feel defeated, and vodka or wine—or both—were especially comforting when I felt that way in the past. Since that is no longer an option, I just feel hopeless.

This brings me back to the beginning of this journal. I can't unknow what I know. Alcohol wasn't comforting me. It was killing me. It played its siren song, lured me in, and slowly wreaked havoc. Intellectually, I'm understanding what I'm learning. *Sometimes* during *some days*, I have patience with my heart trying to catch up with my mind. I must keep leaning on God and other resources. If I don't, I am screwed because I am p-o-w-e-r-l-e-s-s.

~13 days sober

Personal Reflection

I am not the first one to go through what I'm going through, obviously. Change is scary. Relinquishing control is terrifying. But to Whom I am giving it . . . He is kind, caring, all-knowing, safe, and all-powerful. There isn't anything or anyone to whom it is better or safer to give control. All I must do is let go, breathe, and trust.

~14 days sober

Does the Caterpillar Know?

Does the caterpillar know it's turning into a butterfly?
A beautiful, free being?
Does it feel fear while cocooning itself in?

"What if I don't make it?"
"What if I don't fulfill my purpose?"

Is it lonely in the cocoon?
Is the silence deafening?
Does it ever wish it could give up, stop the process, and just continue
    being a caterpillar?
Does the caterpillar ever feel a part of something bigger than itself?

Or, does it just feel alone?
Confined to the limits of a solitary existence
Simply going through the motions; directed by instincts
What does the caterpillar feel during its transformation?
What does the caterpillar think during the metamorphosis?

Do its thoughts even matter?
Because it's the actions of a caterpillar that make it a butterfly
Even so, does the caterpillar feel grateful, content, and happy once
    through the process?
Does it take a break from flying and think, *[Exhale]* "This was all
    worth it"?

~17 days sober

I'm Freaking Sober!

It will be worth it," they say.

"Don't quit before the miracle," they say.

Well, you know what? *Fine! OK! Whatever! I'll do it.* So, I'm sober.
I'm freaking sober.

I survived up until day 9 the first time around, before indulging in
my lust towards the poisonous spirits of alcohol. I pray to be guided
by the Holy Spirit, but oh, how my addicted brain and body long for
a different type of spirit!

The night of my lapse, I embarrassed myself (with my family, my
friend, and my sponsor), I wasted money (on food and drink I don't
remember consuming), I tortured my body (I had the shakes the
next day, night sweats the next five nights, and then a headache for
another week), and I made a mess in my home.

Was it worth it? Was it *reallllly* worth it to get blackout drunk to say "goodbye" to alcohol?

Heck no. It was not.

Now, I'm 18 days sober. It's no freaking picnic. It's one of the hardest things I've ever had to do in my entire existence. So yeah, I'm freaking sober.

It isn't a choice I made. It's a choice I'm making. One that my sick mind doesn't agree with half of the time. But, it's still a choice I have to make just the same. Every day, every minute, every second.

The first step is to admit powerlessness. To say, "Screw this!" and then give it all up to God—not give it all to the bottle like I've trained myself to do.

I'm tired all the time. I'm used to tearing myself down with my drinking and alcoholic behaviors. Now, I'm building myself up with my sober choices. That, in and of itself, is triggering. But, nope! I'm mother-freaking sober!

Dear God, I am really struggling. I hope that you see that my intentions are pure and genuine. I've only made it this far with You. Please. Please keep leading the way. I will follow. I may resist, throw a tantrum, and put my head in my hands when I hear the truth, but I will not stop listening. I will not turn off my willingness. I am in this with You. Thank You for Your guidance and blessings thus far. Please, God, may Your will be done . . . not mine.

~19 days sober

Trapped in this Cocoon

In this condition . . .
I'm blind
I'm blind to the outside world
I'm blind to the reasons of what I feel
I'm blind to the answers to my questions
I'm blind to my Higher Power . . .
Trapped in this cocoon

I miss the old me
And the comforts of

When I walked freely,
Saw, ate, and drank as I pleased
And I saw the beauty of the outside world
Direct works from the Lord above

What was so terrible about that way I was?
Why did I even start this transformation?
My body . . . it hurts
My heart won't stop aching
And my mind . . . it never stops racing!

I'm powerless
My only option is to trust the process of what has already begun
But I'm terrified
I don't like this
It's uncomfortable
It's scary and it feels impossible
At the same time . . .
It feels restorative
It feels like I'm fulfilling my purpose

I miss the comforts of being the old me
Before I trapped myself in this cocoon.

But the process has already begun . . .

~23 days sober

What Fills My Cup?

Thirty-seven days ago, vodka or wine filled my cup. They filled my mouth, my body, and my soul. So much so that I don't remember a lot of that night thirty-seven nights ago.

The question remains. What fills my cup now? Ugh. This is a challenging question. My answer *should* be that my cup is full of gratitude and God. While these are contents of my current cup, they are not the only ingredients. It is filled with boredom and discontentment sometimes. Occasionally, it is filled with contentment and joy—but that is less often. This must be because I'm praying less. It's become difficult to remain focused on a single subject. I haven't been feeding and filling the spiritual emptiness part of my disease as frequently and as genuinely.

Someone said in a meeting, "Every time I close the door on reality, it comes in through the window." I can't shut the door on the truth: I abused alcohol, and it abused me. There was no joy there. God is truth, joy, and freedom. Stay in the day. My cup will become filled with peace, joy, and contentment on a regular basis. I have to stay the course. I must trust the process.

~37 days sober

Capsized: Part I

Capsized
In an ocean of alcohol
Determined to stay sober
All I have to do is open my mouth
Point my chin downward
Sweet relief
That simple
Right there
So close
Then,
I'd be floating in more ways than one

Sober, I am
Sober, I must stay

But why?
I pray and pray for sobriety
But the answer seems to be alcohol!
Is God not leading me to my solution?
Is the answer not alcohol?

Anxious, I feel
Thoughts racing
Exerting energy
Keeping my head above my fate

What am I to do . . . out here by myself?
Capsized . . .
Floating . . .
In an ocean of alcohol

God, tell me!
Please, hear me!

Just as I'm ready to give in
Something catches my eye

A life jacket
A new option
A new solution
I swim to it and put it on
Now, I can rest
God heard me
God has me
I can do this . . .
We will do this.

~41 days sober

Life Lessons from Caterpillars

But just how, in these circumstances, does a fellow 'take it easy'? That's what I want to know."[4]

Yes! Exactly what I've been saying! Does a caterpillar truly just rest and let the process happen? From the point of view which I'm going to stubbornly entertain for a moment . . . NO! It doesn't. It engorges itself with food in preparation. It works to build its cocoon. It actively sheds its skin or whatever—that's what it looks like happens in the YouTube videos I've watched of caterpillar → chrysalis → butterfly transformations!

Deep breath.

Now, from a healthier perspective. The caterpillar goes along . . . the caterpillar trusts the process . . . the caterpillar is taking the action it is supposed to take. I don't know if the caterpillar knows the end result. I don't know if it knows it is going to be a butterfly. I honestly do not think it does. Having that much knowledge might deter the caterpillar from ever taking the action needed to change. Change is scary. I think the caterpillar is blessed to know just enough of the

---

4. *Daily Reflections* (2016), p. 73.

journey ahead so that it isn't overwhelmed—so that the journey seems manageable and possible.

Yet again, I need to take note from the caterpillars. One step at a time.

~43 days sober

The Dangers of Emotions

When Depressed:
My skin isn't my own.

When Hypomanic:
I feel great! I can't stand you! I love me! Ugh! I love you!

When Drunk:
Initially: Woohoo! Now, *this* is who *I am!*
Later: This isn't me. I can't keep doing this to myself.

When Hungover:
Initially: Why do I keep doing this to myself?
Later: My soul, body, mind, skin . . . my everything . . . needs another drink.

When Sober:
This skin doesn't belong.

~44 days sober

Parts of Me

How insulting of me to hate myself and my life. I am made in *His* image, after all. But then there are parts of me I love, and there are periods of time in which I genuinely enjoy myself. What if I don't hate myself and I only hate some of the choices I make? But then, why do I make certain choices if I don't hate myself?

~45 days sober

Only the Actor

Plain and simple, the show runs more smoothly, is more popular, has more longevity, and has overall more quality when I allow my Higher

Power to be the Director, Stage Manager, Prop Designer, Music Producer, etcetera.[5] Whereas I am simply the actor, surrendered to the will of God, the Director. I follow orders of what to say, when to say it, where to stand, when to move, and what to wear. When I completely surrender to God, the result is a masterpiece.

When I take control—when I want to be the costume designer, music producer, and stage manager—life looks different. When I take control, I end up drunk on the floor of my kitchen, alternating between making phone calls to my best friend, my worried mother, and the firecracker side of my sponsor before passing out somewhere in my home. But before that, I was having "fun" taking selfies with different filters, eating food I don't remember eating, and losing my phone that was right in front of me.

When I surrender to God, He is in control of all parts of me. When He guides me to be solely the actor, I have employment opportunities and financial gains, I find moments of emotional peace, I feel a greater intensity of positive emotions, I am more social, I feel competent and content, and most importantly, I feel spiritually nourished.

I feel redundant, but it is truth. Life is clearly meant to be lived with God in control and me solely as the actor. I still resist sometimes, and I ask God for assistance with that. I know He will help. He always does.

Day 50! Thanking God and my sponsor!

~50 days sober

One-of-a-Kind and One-and-the-Same

I am an alcoholic. As an alcoholic, I am one and the same with other alcoholics. No uniqueness here about my disease. Any difference I find in myself leads to separation from my alcoholic herd to isolation with the bottle. I am one and the same.

Yesterday, I learned of someone dying from my disease. Since starting the A.A. program, I've heard of a couple of deaths of people I didn't know. Thus far, this person was the closest I've been to knowing someone personally. My friend in A.A., who is very much alive, shared about her friend that had died from *our* disease. A life was now lifeless. That was sad. My friend was hurting. That hurt. Someone

---

5. *Alcoholics Anonymous (4th ed.)*—"*The Big Book*" (2017), p. 60–61. The theme for this chapter is taken from this book.

died from the disease so many of us fight daily. That was sobering and terrifying. I'm grateful my friend chose to reach out instead of drink. I'm grateful she was at a meeting and not isolating. I'm grateful God allowed me to have fifty days of sobriety before learning of this tragedy. My thoughts and prayers go out to the family of the life lost and to my friend.

I am an alcoholic. If I differ myself from the life that was lost, I may lose myself too.

I am bipolar type two. Bipolar II disorder can disguise itself in many ways, such as: being very productive or hyper, simply having the "blues," just being in a bad mood, being "justifiably" irritable, or simply having a couple of bad nights of sleep. However, without intervention, these small shifts lead to the classic symptoms: devastating lows and euphoric highs. Thinking these shifts in mood are characteristic of a typical functioning brain leads to non-compliance with medication and therapy and ultimately to disastrous, life-altering behaviors and decisions. Even if I present uniquely on a certain day, I am one and the same.

Sober or drunk, depressed or hypomanic, I am Jessica Joy Whalen. God designed me with a one-of-a-kind design. I am akin to a snowflake. How do I survive in a world where I am both one-of-a-kind and one-and-the-same? Just as I am a unique snowflake, never to be copied or duplicated, I have commonalities with other snowflakes. I blend in with my piles of snow. One pile is alcoholism, and another is bipolar II disorder, while another is being a mental health professional, and so on and so forth.

At first glance I may seem like others—another server at a restaurant, another member attending an A.A. meeting, another therapist at an agency, or another client in a waiting room. When more attention is paid and more time is spent, the unique qualities God blessed me with become known. Balance is how I survive in this world, not going to extremes (all-or-nothing approach). I must appreciate my differences *and* my similarities—with my alcoholic herd, my mental health needs, and above anything else, I must stay true to myself.

~51 days sober

Acceptance

I t feels good to be home in my home group. I feel stronger this morning. I feel God's timing . . . His divine order . . . His divine timing.

In the past one-to-two weeks, I've experienced some of my highest sober highs yet and some sober struggles. I've had two relapse dreams in the past four days that have sucked. I've clung to my sponsor more lately. I've given myself permission to do so. I usually feel uncomfortable communicating so frequently, like I'm violating a boundary. P is such a blessing. She has helped.

I had a new insight yesterday, a new revelation, and I'm feeling better about reaching my sixty-day milestone tomorrow. I feel more at peace that I've been doing what I've needed to do to be where I am today.

It's incredible to see and understand how I've been an alcoholic my whole life, before alcohol was ever introduced—before I ever put it into my body. I have so much in common with other alcoholics. My feeling so intensely, my tendency to personalize, my hypersensitivity, my tendency to take a long time to get over something, my insecurities and my discomfort in my own skin, my need to be perfect in my actions/morals/performances/roles/etcetera/etcetera/etcetera.

I engaged in self-harm through cutting and gluttony, but alcohol is what I truly wanted. The others were just fillers.

~59 days sober

Day 60

D ay 60
I climb the ladder
Day 60
I step onto the diving board
Day 60
I look down upon the pool of relapse
This pool . . .
This pool is filled to the brim with good times, carelessness, relief,
    and joy
This pool . . .
This pool is mesmerizing . . . and terrifying
Wait

How did I get up here??
Crap!
I need to call my sponsor
Ring, ring—no answer
Ha-ha, what now, suckas?!
I walk closer to the edge
The pool's beauty draws me near
Sponsor calls back
Decline!
I walk to the back of the board
I prepare to run forward
Ready to make my dive
Ahh!
I'm such a rule follower!
I call my sponsor back
"Don't jump, don't jump!" she says
"This pool . . ."
"This pool is filled to the brim with lies, illusions, self-pity, and defeat."
"No, no, it isn't!"
"Yes, yes, it is."
"It wouldn't be that bad. I would be OK."
"It *would* be that bad. You're an alcoholic. I hope you'd find your way
    back out, but once we dive into the pool one more time, we never
    know. If you look closely, you will see others in the pool already.
    Ask them how long they've been there. Make your decision and
    call me back. Bye."
I throw my phone to the ground in anger and rebellion
Is this truth she speaks?
I sit on the diving board and closely examine the pool below me
First glance
I see no one, I see nothing
She was wrong! Ha! Time to dive!
As I stand and prepare for my victorious dive, I see movement
I pause
I wait for another sign of life
Thirty seconds later I see a face appear from the murky mixture of
    alcohol
A man
A man takes a breath and again disappears into the depths
I scurry off the board and down the ladder

Filled with confusion and concern
I wait for the person to come up for air once more
Here he is!
"Sir! Sir! Are you OK?"
"Yeahhh, man! Why wouldn't I be? This party is lit!" the man
     exclaims as he sinks into the depths once more
Party? Whatever did he mean?
I have my question ready for when he takes his next breath
He surfaces . . .
"Sir! What do you mean, 'party'?"
"The party down below! You should join!"
"There are others?"
"Look around! Mostly everyone just breathes through straws, so they
     don't have to surface. I don't know if it's because I'm new, but I
     don't mind coming back up for air."
And back down he goes
Perplexed, I look around . . .
My gosh, are these cocktail straws?
It appears to be the ends of black cocktail straws, emerging from the
     murky alcoholic mixture
How much oxygen can a person possibly be inhaling at one time?
My new informant friend emerges yet again . . .
"Sir! How long have you been here?"
"Not too long. Only one week . . . or two weeks . . . something like that."
"What about the others, the ones with the straws?"
"It varies, really. Anywhere from a few months to a few decades.
     When are you coming in?"
"I'm still thinking about it. Do the others *ever* come to the surface?"
My voice cracks as I continue to search for hope in my plan to relapse
"I haven't seen anyone surface yet. They say there is nothing left for
     them up here."
I go to ask another question, but away he goes
I understand . . .
Our disease is calling him down

I only want to take a dip into the pool
Now I'm scared I will get trapped inside forever
What should I do?
I sit there

Scared to even dangle my toe
My informant friend doesn't acknowledge me anymore, as he has
    only one thing on his mind
Sitting there, I realize
It *is* truth
This pool . . .
This pool is only filled with lies and illusions of a good time
If I dive and never leave the pool . . .
I will be leaving everything I have outside of the pool
My skin, my eyes, my organs . . . everything will decline and decay
I will feel nothing but defeat and self-pity
I search for my phone, sure that it is in pieces
Miraculously, it is not
God protected it
I'm able to call my sponsor to say I'm not taking the dive today
Day 60
I looked into the pool of relapse and reconsidered
Day 60
I stepped back from the diving board
Day 60
I climbed down the ladder
Day 60
I surrendered to God and chose sobriety

                         ~60 days sober

Humility

*A fellow A.A. member I had become friends with was going through a
divorce and needed a place to stay temporarily while she finalized her
housing situation. The plan was for her to rent a room in my home for
as long as she needed. She had nearly 10 years of sobriety while I was
struggling to maintain 2 months of sobriety. I shared my Day 60 with her,
and it made her reconsider.*

Holy crap
This is really happening
To go from being mindful of the high-risk elements in my life
To go from dodging, escaping, and cutting out those elements from
    my life . . .

I'm the high-risk variable in someone else's
I'm the factor to consider
I could be of harm to someone
To someone's mental stability . . . to their recovery . . . to their sobriety
I'm the contents of the container with the skull and crossbones
I'm what's inside the room entered only with hazmat suits
I am someone else's high-risk factor . . . despite my own progressions
     in recovery
This is not written in self-pity
This is written only in reality . . . in humility

~62 days sober

Existence

My existence has become an oscillation
Between thriving and merely surviving
Gratitude and self-pity
Surrender and self-will
Between giving up control and taking it back
Depression
Oh, the history we share
How I have loved you and how I have loathed you
Such comfort in your wicked ways
With your suffocating silence
And your iron grip
Who and what is more powerful than you?
Alcohol!
I trained myself to reach for the bottle
The sky at night became brighter with the substance
The weight of the day became lighter when I knew I could come
     home to the bottle
I thought I figured out how to manage you, depression
We could finally coexist!
How naïve
This was just another trick
If I partied with alcohol at night
It stole the following day
I fell for this trick day after day
Month after month
Until I was more broken than before I ever picked up the bottle

You tricked me into feeling a new type of low
You tricked me into developing a new type of problem
I tricked myself
More than ever
I'm in need of something larger
Not a greater buzz
Not a stronger escape
I need something that can carry all of this and more
I need my Savior

God,
Please grant me the serenity to accept the things I cannot change
The courage to change the things that I can
And the wisdom to know the difference
If I am meant to feel what I am feeling
Please help me maintain willingness to experience this with humility, not self-will
Help me stay connected to You
Help me stay connected with the truth and not lose my way in the darkness
You are the Way, the Truth, and the Life
I know this, and I believe it with my heart, my mind, and my soul
But my disease feeds me lies, and I often feel so weak
It encourages me to go down paths that do not lead to You
If I were to listen to the lies
I know You would still love me and accept me
Even before I'm ready to turn back to You
Even so, I truly don't want to go down them, Lord
Please, "relieve me of the bondage of self," that I may better do Thy will [6]
May Your will be done, not mine
I love You, Father
In your name I pray,
Amen

~67 days sober

---

6. *Alcoholics Anonymous (4th Ed)*—*"The Big Book"* (2017). Part of the Step 3 prayer on p. 63.

Relapse: DAY 1, TAKE 3

Is it true what I have done?
I chose my addiction over my Higher Power?
I gave into the lies

I turned my back from His grace
I knew myself to be weak
I knew myself to be manipulated
Stubborn, I am
Stubborn, I stay
Take 1
Take 2
Take 3
Sober 9 days
Sober 67 days
Sober 1 day
What is even the point anymore?
Alcohol!
I know you to be manipulative
I know you to be cunning and powerful[7]
I know I am simply your prey
I know I am not a victim
You do not come uninvited
You give life
You give joy
You give fun
For as much as you give, you also take
You suck
You lie
You kill
You've overstayed your welcome

~1 day sober

---

7. *Alcoholics Anonymous (4th ed.)*—*"The Big Book"* (2017), pp. 58–59.

Relapse Continues: 24 HOURS SOBER

(First Meeting Since Relapse)

- All I have to do is admit that I am powerless and then B-E-L-I-E-V-E.
- All I have to do is believe. Believe in God. T-R-U-S-T.
- *His* will. His plan. *His* process. Not mine. I am P-O-W-E-R-L-E-S-S.
- I must ride this journey ONE-DAY-AT-A-TIME.
- It is progress, N-O-T perfection.
- NOT white chip of shame . . . white chip of H-O-P-E.
- No more justifications, just T-R-U-T-H.
- Go to meetings, talk to other alcoholics, talk to my sponsor, and, most importantly, talk to G-O-D.

~1 day sober

The Dive

Day 60, I walked away from the pool. Day 60, I felt good about my decision. Intellectually, I understood the lies of the pool. Emotionally, my heart continued to hurt. I continued to long for what I deemed forbidden. But walked away, I did. I told God I chose Him. And, I continued to choose Him for the next several days until I found myself back at the pool on Day 67, contemplating.

My thoughts consumed me. Is it *really* filled with lies, illusions, self-pity, and defeat? *Or,* is it filled with good times, carelessness, relief, and joy? I genuinely remember good times of carelessness and joy! Even so, this doesn't feel right. *Why* did I walk back here?

This is not OK! What is happening? Why am I taking off my shoes? I needn't dangle my toe! *You just need to see how it feels again.* NO! NO! I can't. *Yes, yes you can.* NO! Oh, wow. It smells so good. Am I really doing this? No, no, no. God, help me, please! *Why say His name? You know you stopped relying on Him. Look at you, rolling up your pant legs as you cry out His name. You want this pool more than you want Him.* I mustn't. *Only a toe, that's all.*

There I went, about to act on my relapse with "only a toe." With such intention, I balanced myself on my left foot and slowly lowered my right foot towards the murky depths. Breathing ever so slowly. Heart racing. As contact was about to be made, I placed my right foot back down on the pavement, bent my knees, and then pushed off with both feet.

Perfect dive. Relapse.

~2 days sober

Day 67

Submerged. No turning back now. First, I sip. I think, *Not quite the same taste as I remember.* Second, I gulp. I no longer pay attention to taste. I am only chasing feelings. Gulp, gulp, gulp. Drinking as if someone is going to snatch me. Can't breathe. I return to the top for air.

At the surface, gasping. I'm closer to the straws down here. There are more than I previously thought. I wonder for a second if I'll need a straw for myself, if I'll ever make it back out, or if I'm in for good. Then I think, *Why am I thinking when I could be drinking?* Down I go.

I drink. And drink more. I have a feeling my time is limited—like it has an expiration date. I return to the surface for air. Confused between right and wrong. Between self-will and surrender. I call out to my sponsor to inform her of my latest dive.

She appears. She reminds me I had a choice in making the dive. Keeping myself afloat, I listen. I have nothing to say. How can I down here? She says if I'm in the pool, we are not to talk. She walks away. I wonder if my bleeding heart will bloody the water. I slip back into the depths. Down below, I don't drink, I only think. I've created this. A situation in which I feel self-pity and shame. Still, zero consumption. I dodge the bodies of the others and return to the surface. What have I done?

I swim to the side, and with all my might I pull myself out. I lay on the cement, drenched in my relapse.

Hours pass. I resist re-entry. I call again for my sponsor. No response. I understood. Wallowing in my shame of disappointing myself and others, of the harm I put myself in, and how I jeopardized everything by diving—I fall asleep. Day 67 is finally over.

Day 1. Starting over. A brand-new day. A brand-new beginning. Hopeful. I can do this. I stay out of the pool. Yet, I don't leave the poolside.

Day 2. I speak with my sponsor: "I'm OK! How are you? This is my second day out of the pool! I've learned my lesson!" Even so, I still don't leave.

Hours later, the vodka and the wine from the murky depths call my name. I resist. I distract. I rationalize.

Alas, I'm seduced back into the pool. Relapse.

Day 1. I wake up outside the pool. I'm not sure if I hurt more physically or emotionally. Sweaty, anxious, transparent. "Don't be an alcoholic, don't be an alcoholic, don't be an alcoholic." This mantra runs through my head as I circle the outskirts of the pool. Just take a left and leave!

I make a right. Splish, splash. Back in the pool, but my feelings continue to worsen. No relief felt! I feel like I'm dying. My stomach. My head. My cravings. My disease! Why do I keep jumping in? *Why?*

Back under I go. Gulp. Gulp. Gulp. I arise for air when the pain becomes too great. Then re-submerge once the pain eases. My method is starting not to work. The pain is becoming too much. Everything is hazy.

Day 1. I wake up halfway inside and halfway outside of the pool. Acid reflux. Indigestion. I honestly think I can breathe fire. This must STOP. Still, I can't ignore, I'm still halfway inside the pool.

Conflicted. I'm in fear of losing what I have outside of the pool, but also scared of not getting what I want that is inside the pool . . . ever again. But, am I benefiting from these murky depths? I feel like I'm dying. I battle. I think. I breathe. I pray.

I compromise. As I remove myself from the pool, I allow the drippings from my fingers to fall into my mouth. I remove my clothes, hold them up high, and wring them out so that I may drink what falls from them.

Standing outside of the pool. Naked. Vulnerable. Miserable. Terrified. Exhausted. I realize that if I don't reconnect to the world outside of the pool now, I'm going to dive back in.

I take a left and leave. I shower the stink of my disease off me. I put on clean clothes. I call my sponsor to tell her no more diving.

Day 2. I make it to a meeting. I pick up a white chip of hope. This is the start of my new beginning.

~4 days sober

Meeting Reflection

Someone shared, "My disease is out there doing push-ups . . . just waiting."

- Sober or drunk. Drinking water or drinking vodka. Sober 1 day or sober 67 days . . . I am an alcoholic.
- Sober or drunk. Drinking water or drinking vodka. Sober 1 day or sober 67 days . . . God is my Higher Power. Praying or not. He is still there, always.
- Sober or drunk. Drinking water or drinking vodka. Sober 1 day or sober 67 days. . . Alcohol is stronger now than it was when I last drank it seven days ago. This is terrifying! But I needn't be scared because God is *always* stronger. And my disease is a devil.

~7 days sober

Alcohol

Once full of seasons
Now only consists of one
When did you start hating me?
I pledged my allegiance
I pledged my loyalty
Then your true colors showed through

What once was bright
And full of color
Turned dark
Black, grey, charcoal . . . anything to block the light
Little did I realize, you were an extension of me
How much harder I've been making my own path

How much of a strain I've been adding
I'm full of despair!

I separate from you
I leave you behind
It's brighter in the present with you in the past
It's lighter up here, now that I've lessened my burden
But the problem remains . . .
Myself
The reason I reached for you in the first place

~9 days sober

The Pink Cloud

The pink cloud[8] has lifted and floated away
Up, up and away
There goes my confidence, or illusion thereof
I'm left with defects of self
Defects of character
What am I to do with these?
These traits which led me to loneliness, guilt, and shame . . . and
    eventually to the restlessness, irritability, and discontentment[9]
The drink is no longer the solution
My Higher Power is
There is still something I'm missing
There is still something I'm not doing
I'm going to relapse again if I don't catch it
"I need to remember each day that deceiving myself about myself is
    setting myself up for failure and disappointment in life and in
    A.A."[10]

~14 days sober

Fear

Fear blocks my—will. If I ever have something blocking me from
an achievement, a social engagement, a personal growth, a next step,

---

8. "A new lifestyle of sobriety is refreshing, which can result in a natural
high during the early days and weeks of sobriety. People sometimes call this
the 'pink cloud.'" From https://eudaimoniahomes.com/recovery/what-is-
the-pink-cloud/.
9. *Alcoholics Anonymous (4th ed.)*—"*The Big Book*" (2017), p. xxviii.
10. *Daily Reflections* (2016), p. 117.

a decision, etcetera, it is fear. Thankfully, I am good at practicing something I am motivated to achieve. I am OK with applying hard work and determination. I am OK (most of the time) with not receiving instant results as long as I have an understanding that results will occur in the future.

At my latest job, I have been told that I am patient and a hard worker. Both are truths. I have also been told that I am quiet and that I do not talk a lot. That can be very true of my personality, but it can also be true of my character defects of isolating and withdrawing from the social aspect of work.

Sobriety is challenging on a deeper level. In the 12 steps of A.A., only the first step mentions alcohol. As people in the rooms say, "I came to A.A. to get help with my drinking, but I stayed to get help with my thinking." They call it "stinkin' thinkin.'"

Sobriety is not mastering a skill. It is progress, not perfection. It is not a new job for which I go to an orientation and then go through some training. In sobriety, the training never ends. I think I find discouragement in that sometimes. Do I also feel fear? Fear that I won't last? Fear that I will give up on myself? I don't know. But whatever it is, I am asking God daily to "relieve me of the bondage of self, that I may better do [His] will."[11]

Please, take my life and my will, God. Guide me in my recovery. Show me how to live. Your will, not mine. Amen.

~17 days sober

New Soil . . . New Roots

Daily Reflection: April 22

"Moments of perception can build into a lifetime of spiritual serenity, as I have excellent reason to know. Roots of reality, supplanting the neurotic underbrush, will hold fast despite the high winds of the forces which would destroy us, or which we would use to destroy ourselves."

I came to A.A. green—a seedling quivering with exposed taproots. It was for survival, but it was a beginning. I

11. *Alcoholics Anonymous (4ᵗʰ ed.)*—"*The Big Book*" (2017). Part of the Step 3 prayer on p. 63.

stretched, developed, twisted, but with the help of others, my spirit eventually burst up from the roots. I was free. I

acted, withered, went inside, prayed, acted again, understood anew, as one moment of perception struck. Up from my roots, spirit-arms lengthened into strong, green shoots: high-springing servants stepping skyward.

"Here on earth God unconditionally continues the legacy of higher love. My A.A. life put me 'on a different footing . . . [my] roots grasped a new soil.'"[12]

This reflection currently describes my soul. It describes my process of transforming from a caterpillar to a butterfly. The old me is withering away—old ways of pleasure, old ways of harm. I am learning how to be new. I am eager, willing, resistant, and terrified at the same time. Thank God I have a God.

~18 days sober

Balance

It has been easy in the past (and present) to label myself as *bad* instead of *wrong*. I feel I always *should know better*, but most times, I truly do my best for what I know in that given moment. I am learning that I do not need to shame myself for not forgiving myself. I need to follow through with what I preach to others (i.e., clients), to be easy on myself, to keep it simple, and then *maybe* I can forgive myself.

"Deprivation and overconsumption are flip sides of the same coin. The point of recovery is finding balance."[13] For at least the past fifteen years of my life, I have tried to fill the hole in me through deprivation or overconsumption—especially when it comes to my body and my body image. Ugh, I hate talking about body image. Last fall, my counselor, X, pointed out my tendency to be all-or-nothing. With my thinking, I tend to be black-or-white, in-or-out, no grey, no middle

---

12. *Daily Reflections* (2016), p. 125. First paragraph is a quote from *As Bill Sees It* (2001), p. 173. The second paragraph is the reflection. The third is from *Alcoholics Anonymous (4th ed.)—"The Big Book"* (2017), p. 12.
13. *Drop the Rock* (2005), p. 6.

ground. The coin of deprivation and overconsumption is extremely relevant to me. *I need* balance.

~18 days sober

Which Pen Will I Pick Up Today?

I am the author of my own life, of my own misery. My actions either hurt or help. My God is a pen I choose to write with on some days. The days that I work the A.A. program, the days I surrender. I write with the pen of God. When I write with this holy pen, I still have fears, I still have doubts, and I still try to manipulate the words I write with a self-pitying undertone. But, with this pen, I can ask God to change my writing, to allow me to write in humility. To help me write in alignment with His will.

Do I get tired of writing with this pen? His pen? Because I put it down sometimes to pick up the pen of self-destruction. This pen fits comfortably in my hand. It has grooves in all the right places. My hand has calluses from using this pen so often. I then write my tales of isolation, gluttony, and self-destruction. It is easier to put down the pen of God than it is to put down the pen of self-destruction. Just as it is harder to pick up the pen of God than the pen of self-destruction on some days.

Life happens one day at a time. Which pen will I pick up today?

~19 days sober

In Between

Floating in between. New ways are hard to maintain and have fleeting, yet incredible, satisfaction. Previous self-destructive behaviors are now empty, bringing no joy, not even temporarily. I have realized that the anticipation of the destructive behavior was the joy, not the act itself.

In between my old self and my new. The caterpillar has completed the physical changes of turning into a butterfly, but the process has yet to be completed.

~20 days sober

Happiness Is Not the Point
Daily Reflection: April 26

"I don't think happiness or unhappiness is the point. How do we meet the problems we face? How do we best learn from them and transmit what we have learned to others, if they would receive the knowledge?"

In my search "to be happy," I changed jobs, married and divorced, took geographical cures, and ran myself into debt—financially, emotionally and spiritually. In A.A., I'm learning to grow up. Instead of demanding that people, places and things make me happy, I can ask God for self-acceptance. When a problem overwhelms me, A.A.'s Twelve Steps will help me grow through the pain. The knowledge I gain can be a gift to others who suffer with the same problem. As Bill said, "When pain comes, we are expected to learn from it willingly, and help others to learn. When happiness comes, we accept it as a gift, and thank God for it." (*As Bill Sees It*, p. 306)[14]

"When a problem overwhelms me, A.A.'s 12 Steps will help me grow through the pain." *Through* the pain—not *avoiding* the pain, not *stopping midway* through, not *pretending the pain doesn't exist. Through* the pain.

As the title states, "Happiness is not the point." Neither is unhappiness. Again, screw my feelings, they aren't facts. The point is to make it *through* the pain by relying on God and what the 12 Steps have taught me and are still teaching me. Survive and learn from the pain with a willing attitude, and then pass the message to others. And, hey, if happiness does come, enjoy it! Because it is a true blessing from God. Thank God for it.

This reflection is humorous in an ironic way because I thought lasting happiness is what I've been after. Not supercharged joy, not out-of-this-world bliss, but reasonable happiness. *But*, happiness is not the point. I think I knew this, but, at the same time, I hadn't quite put

14. *Daily Reflections* (2016), p. 125. First paragraph is a quote from *As Bill Sees It* (2001), p. 306. The second paragraph is the reflection.

the concept together yet. I'm changing into a butterfly. Little, if any, have I spoken of the butterfly's happiness. I've mostly spoken of the divine metamorphosis that occurs both inside and out to become a butterfly. I do believe the gift of happiness comes from God and through the metamorphosis that takes place in the ongoing practice of the 12 Steps—and the gratitude thereof. So, happiness is possible, but it is not the point.

~22 days sober

Alcohol-is-m

Living with the disease of alcoholism
Living with a disease without a cure
A cure means a treatment plan
A plan with a start, middle, and end
Treatment with a termination date
To then move forward,
To continue to live life
Living with a disease where only a daily reprieve is possible
Alcoholism can never be cured
Never going into remission
It is alcohol-is-m
Not, alcohol-was-m
I'm rebuilding myself from within to live life 24 hours at a time
To not borrow from tomorrow
To not live in the past
But to live in the present
One freaking day at a time

~24 days sober

Cup

Drink in hand
Come at me, world
Empty cup in hand
Hold on, world
No cup in hand

How can I manage the world?
I must find my cup
I must refill my cup
Then I can manage the world
And myself within
But sober,
What do I fill my cup with?

~24 days sober

Inner Peace

The answer is within, deep inside. It is not in the world. It is not of the world. It is spiritual. My God made me imperfectly perfect. He made me in His image. Why is it so hard to love what He made with such intention? The *why* does not really matter. I am just so stubborn, and I want to understand everything. I must divorce parts of myself I have long been accustomed to—self-centeredness and self-pity. Me, myself, and I. I have a good heart; I really should use it more with others. I have hated my body for so long; it is time to love it—not briefly but long term. I need to let go of all the poison. Inner peace is what I crave. Inner peace is what I want. But, ultimately, may Thy will be done,[15] not mine.

~29 days sober

4th Step, Take 2

Lord,

I must make the right choices in my life. But, good grief, I need Your help in doing so. Because this morning, You are telling me (again, and very bluntly) that if I make the right choices, the "inner dictatorship of habits slowly [loses] its grip."[16] I am all ears for this message right now. I am so tired of these old habits, these memories of the past, and these worn-out cycles of behavior. I know, "If I seek [You], I can find a better way to live."[17] Please help me to do that now and to be easy on myself. I love You.

Amen.

---

15. *Alcoholics Anonymous (4th ed.)*—*"The Big Book"* (2017). Part of the Step 3 prayer on p. 63.
16. *Daily Reflections* (2016), p. 135.
17. Ibid.

P.S. Please guide me to be honest when I do my fourth step again—in ways I wasn't when I did my first fourth step. Life is already giving me situations in which to practice honesty (for example, when the world has tried twice to give me money—fraudulently—that wasn't mine. I returned to it both times to remain honest with myself and honest with You). Please help me dig within myself to be honest about things I usually keep hidden. Please prepare my sponsor to hear me. Please assist her in guiding me through this next step. I am worn out by the inner dictatorship of my habits. You are my Coach, my Captain, and my Leader. Please help me in finding ways to continue to surrender all parts of me to You, Almighty God. If I am a candy bar, I want You to be the caramel filling! I am just a vessel for You. In Your name I pray, Amen.

~32 days sober

To Have It All

To have It All, every day
To then have Nothing in an instant
To rationalize that a drink would bring back having It All
To have knowledge a drink would resolve nothing but destroy Everything
To have humility to reconsider
To have the will to surrender to Him
To remain sober and realize,
It All is *still* there

~34 days sober

Overdosed

Today, I was told my A.A. buddy's stepdaughter overdosed last night. She passed away. Reportedly, she appeared to be sleeping, and her son went to wake her up—but she never woke up. *She will never wake up again.* My A.A. friend is already going through a tough time personally, and now this. My heart hurts for her, for her husband, and for her family. I will pray for their sobriety.

Me . . . this scares *me*. It reminds me of the time I was passed out on my bed, black-out drunk, and I could not be woken up. Phone calls, music blaring, dogs barking, doorbell ringing—nothing. After a while, I finally came to, but I was disoriented. I did not know what time it was. I did not know what day it was.

This tragedy also reminds me of a customer I served yesterday at work. She had yellow eyes. My sponsor talks about having yellow eyes before she went to an alcohol detox facility. When I relapsed a month ago, my sponsor said if I continued drinking the way I was, I was headed to a detox facility myself. So was I headed towards having yellow eyes? Was I headed towards not being able to be woken up?

Lord, may Your will be done. Amen.

~35 days sober

Fear Is a Mile Wide

"Fear is a mile wide but only an inch thick. You just need to punch through it and realize it's not so bad."
—A.A. Member

~35 days sober

The Voice in My Head

I have always been taught about God—His capabilities, how to trust Him, how to include Him—but I am realizing I have never known how to *truly* rely on Him. Has it been my fear of giving up control? Has it been a fear of giving control to something I cannot see? Have I been scared that I am not worthy to give up my problems to someone so mighty? I don't know. All I know is that I have never known how to fully rely on God and *fully surrender as a continued state of being*. I have known how to surrender but only in moments. That is still me controlling everything, isn't it?

~37 days sober

Sober Relationships

I feel . . .
Itchy
Anxious
Furious
Restless
Discontented
Irritable
Un-soothed
Untamed
Craving
Confused

I have . . .
Needs
Wants
Desires
Unrealistic expectations

~37 days sober

Quid Pro Quo

Quid pro quo. This for that. That is how and what my life had become. Grueling day at work? I earned a drink. Helped a friend? Good thing happened? Let's celebrate with a drink! Crappy thing happened? Bad thing probably going to happen? I *deserve* a drink. Quid pro quo. This for that. *This* for alcohol. *That* for a drink. This was my *rational* thinking pattern for a long time.

Now, I am sober. What do I get in return? What am I getting for this and for that? Gratitude? Positive emotions? Service work to other people and that's it? Seriously?

The moral of the story, as is the moral to every freaking story in A.A. (and life, I am learning), is that I needn't have expectations—of any kind. Do something to do it. If I am still to expect something, expect nothing back in return. Don't be a selfish alcoholic. Just be. Serve others. Care for self. Keep it simple. Or as they lovingly say in A.A., "Keep it simple, stupid."

~37 days sober

Rolling with It vs. Getting Rolled Over

Rolling with It	*Getting Rolled Over*
• Go with the flow • Be flexible • Don't overthink it • Let it go • Relax • Suck it up • Breathe • Be positive • Be present • Focus on the now • Don't make it harder than it has to be	• Blame myself • Feel guilt • Isolate and sulk • Fine, whatever • Escape, escape, escape • Alcohol • Never deal • Tuck tail • I don't care anyways • It doesn't matter • It hurts too much • Escape, escape, escape • Alcohol • Past • Present • Doesn't matter • It all hurts • Escape, escape, escape • Alcohol

~37 days sober

Quotes from the Room of A.A.

"Never give up based on your experience."

"Experience alone is not enough to change behavior. Evaluated behavior is enough. I need to look at my underlying defects."

"The only way I can make it through the day is to remember who I am: an alcoholic."

"Becoming right-sized (who you're meant to be) is humility."

"Share your troubles, they're halved. Share your joys, they're doubled."

—Quotes from the members of A.A.

I am powerless over alcohol. Am I powerless over my emotions too? I. Am. An. Alcoholic. I. Am. An. Alcoholic. I. Am. An. Alcoholic. I. Am. An. Alcoholic. I. Am. Powerless. I. Am. Powerless. I. Am. Powerless. I. Am. An. Alcoholic. I. Am. A. Powerless. Alcoholic. I. Am. A. Powerless. Alcoholic. I. Am. A. Powerless. Alcoholic.

I am powerless over everything, *right?* But I still *have to* take action. Expectations lead to disappointments. Disappointments lead to resentments. Expectations lead to disappointments. Disappointments lead to resentments. Expectations lead to disappointments. Disappointments lead to resentments. I. Am. An. Alcoholic. I. Am. An. Alcoholic. I. Am. An. Alcoholic.

The only thing that can fill my alcoholic void is God. But I am an alcoholic who wants *instant* results. I am feeling things so strongly. I want to be divorced from these feelings—*now.* Prayer is powerful. Sometimes I even feel immediate relief but other times, not as much. I *know* God is always working, whether immediate results occur or not. I do not want to drink. I want to find an alternative. A loophole. Something to help bring relief until I feel God's results.

How selfish of me. How impatient. How not trusting of me. I don't know! I am just writing how I feel even though I know it is completely wrong. Thus, if I know what is wrong, I know what is right. I know the answer: God. Turn to Him. More than ever before. *I just feel!*

~38 days sober

Born to Be Ill

Born to be ill
Born—not to be the illest, but simply ill
Born to be tormented by terrors inside and out

Born with white eyes destined to be yellow

Born with a liver waiting for cirrhosis
Born with a heart meant to be tachycardic
Born with a brain wanting to die

Born with a temperament full of fear and depressive to the touch
Born with moods that swing from side to side
Born to blame self, even hurt self, before others
Born with my heart on my sleeve, then live to second guess my actions

Born hypersensitive to anything and everything
Born to self-loathe, to wallow in shame
Born to morbidly reflect[18] on yesterdays
Born in need of an attitude adjustment

Born with a life
Born with love
Born with opportunities
Born with a path

Born with strength
Born with courage
Born with patience
Born with conviction, pushing me to be honest at every turn

Born with both defects and assets of character
Born fallible but amenable
Born with a God with only assets
Born with a God who has a plan for me
Born with a God whose love for me is relentless
Born blessed

~39 days sober

Freedom To Be Me

Daily Reflection: May 18th

Yes! Lord! This is such a true freedom. I D-O-N-T H-A-V-E T-O D-R-I-N-K T-O-D-A-Y. My face and heart both smile. They match my genuine desire *not* to drink. Amen, Lord!

"I had a new freedom today, the freedom to be me. I have the freedom to be the best me I have ever been."[19] *Wow.* I have the *freedom* to be

18. *Alcoholics Anonymous (4th ed.)— "The Big Book"* (2017), p. 86.
19. *Daily Reflections* (2016), p. 147.

me. Me . . . the intuitive smart aleck. The silly-serious person I am. The person *You* created.

An important reminder of an A.A promise was pointed out in today's reflection: "If we are painstaking about this phase of our development, we will be amazed before we are halfway through. We are going to know a new freedom and a new happiness."[20] I must stay the course. My course has had some highs and lows lately, but true to the course I have stayed! I am grateful to God. Thank You, Lord. May *Your* will be done, not mine.

~44 days sober

Personal Reflection

Thank You, Lord, that this program and the recovery community is turning "me" into "we." It's something I've always known in one way or another—the "we" of being part of a sports team. The "we" of being part of a family. The "we" of a friendship or relationship (healthy and unhealthy). But, in all these examples, I still felt alone. I still felt, "I." Not in a healthy way—as in, I am my own independent person contributing to the whole—but in a secluded, misunderstood, me vs. the world type of way.

From the beginning, both this program and my sponsor have been teaching me lessons about "we." But it has only been in recent weeks that I am understanding how my sobriety depends on it. Also, how I'm healthier and happier for it.

I want to be done with this type of soul-sickness[21] and what my sponsor has called *spiritual selfishness* because those things bind me to the bottle. I want to improve my existing relationships but also build new ones. Whatever His will is for me, I want to do that! It's *much* better than my will.

~48 days sober

Meeting Reflection

- "I was looking for external solutions for internal problems."
- "No 'thing' can make me happy."

---

20. *Alcoholics Anonymous (4ᵗʰ ed.)*—"*The Big Book*" (2017), p. 83. A quote from *Daily Reflections* (2016).
21. *Twelve Steps and Twelve Traditions* (2017), p. 44.

- "I appreciate the sun coming up in the morning instead of dreading it."
- "Money doesn't buy happiness; it just makes the misery less painful."
- "Desiring it is not the same thing as getting it."[22]

~49 days sober

Need. Surrender. Will.

Lord,

I need You in my life right now.

Yes. I need You. I am always aware of my need for You. I try to practice the action of needing You and the action of having You simply out of the knowledge that I need You all day, every day. But right now, right now, I feel the need. I feel the emptiness. I feel my disease moving and spreading inside of me. I can hear it taunting me.

I feel the truth. The truth that is You. The truth that I need You. I need You to fill me. I also feel my urges to resist. I feel my desires to push away, to push away from Your truth. The times I am weak enough and I do turn away, I thrust myself back to You, my Creator. You are the only way through these thoughts and feelings. You are the only way to the other side. You are my Almighty. My Director. My Stage Manager. My Shepherd.[23]

Maybe I am meant to be feeling what I am. Or maybe a character defect of mine is going on a joy ride and it is creating space between You and me. Even so, I painfully recognize my need for You.

I surrender. Completely. I surrender my all so that I may better do Your will. Please, please, draw me near as my self-will has taken me places beyond Your intention and beyond my understanding. "Relieve me of the bondage of self, that I may better do Thy will."[24] May I do Your will always. In Your name I pray, Father.

Amen.

~49 days sober

---

22. Quotes from A.A. members.
23. *Alcoholics Anonymous (4ᵗʰ ed.)*—"*The Big Book*" (2017), p. 60–61.
24. *Alcoholics Anonymous (4ᵗʰ ed.)*—"*The Big Book*" (2017). Part of the Step 3 prayer on p. 63.

The Beer Cooler

Like a sci-fi movie of being exposed to a contaminant—where a visual is given of the contaminant penetrating the skin, entering the blood vessels, circulating the bloodstream, and reaching its way to the brain. It's as though I've felt the emotional manipulation . . . the emotional poison (the one hundred forms of fear[25]) of my disease set in this week just like I'm describing it.

Last night I had a breakdown at the restaurant where I am a server. I sell wine and other alcoholic beverages semi-often. I had become accustomed to it to the point that it hasn't been triggering. But last night, after having already served alcoholic beverages that evening, I inhaled a tantalizing scent as I picked up a glass of chardonnay from the bar to deliver to a table. When I used to drink, I loved wine but never chardonnay. I thought sipping chardonnay was like licking the inside of a wooden barrel. Gross. But, last night, that glass of chardonnay smelled like what I imagine a flower from the Garden of Eden smelled like. Heavenly.

It did not make me want to drink. But it did make me lose my mind. My boss is a recovering addict, so I went to find her. With tears in my eyes, I said, "I smelled wine." She told me to take a break in the cooler and a manager would handle my tables. I went to the cooler which, ironically, was a beer cooler, and I had zero cell service. I just cried and cried. I told God I needed Him. I surrendered to Him and I asked for His will to be done. I asked Him to please "relieve me of the bondage of self."[26] I repeated this over and over. God heard me. Suddenly, I had cell service. I called my sponsor and was able to talk to her. P heard my panic but talked me through my fears. I survived the night. I stayed sober.

Looking back, I can see how I was driven by my one hundred forms of fear, just as "The Big Book" says. I am extremely humbled and grateful for this experience that allowed me to practice humility, surrendering, and reconnecting with my Higher Power.

~52 days sober

---

25. *Alcoholics Anonymous (4th ed.)*—*"The Big Book"* (2017), p. 62.
26. *Alcoholics Anonymous (4th ed.)*—*"The Big Book"* (2017). Part of the Step 3 prayer on p. 63.

The Path

In graduate school, a classmate told me a metaphor for understanding and respecting the multiple religious practices of spirituality that exist in the world. He described it like a mountain—and that God (or *a god*) was at the top of this mountain. Every religion or spirituality starts at the base and climbs up the mountain using *their own unique path* to find a god of their understanding. The beauty of this metaphor is that regardless of the path and the motive, the intent and purpose is to climb to the top and find their higher power. Every tribe and organization busy climbing their own unique path may understand God differently and worship Him differently than those climbing next to them.

The reflection this morning stated, "It is a new path, one that leads to infinite light at the top of the mountain."[27] It is in reflecting upon this that I realize I am no longer part of the non-denominational Christianity group that is climbing the mountain towards God. I chose months ago to walk away from them. I did not walk away from God, just the group. I realized with the group that I was going through the motions and my personal relationship with God was shallow. Thus, I decided to climb the mountain on my own.

Since going out on my own—well, of course I'm not truly alone because God is with me—I've had time to pray, reflect, and meditate. I've had time to understand God differently. I'm climbing my own path up the mountain, one path special between me and my Creator. Once I reach the top, I know my God will not only accept me, but He will embrace me.

~59 days sober

Eyes of an Addict

Waiting for the next dose
Waiting to be brought back to life
These lifeless eyes
These eyes of an addict

When I'm sober
I feel it in my eyes

27. *Daily Reflections* (2016), p. 162.

They feel without
They match my soul

When alcohol circulates my veins
My eyes are uniquely pressurized
They feel alive

When alcohol has been detoxed
My eyes deflate
They are lifeless, heavy
Dark circles weigh below them
Waiting, just waiting, to be brought back to life

~61 days sober

I Am Co-Occurring

I am co-occurring
I happen simultaneously, all at once

Like a yolk separate from the white,
I try to split the two
But I am meant to coexist

I am co-occurring
I happen simultaneously, all at once

Paralyzed between my disorders
I find strength regardless
I fight one of my tormentors
But I am left defenseless to my other plight

I am co-occurring
I happen simultaneously, all at once

The message is clear
Both afflictions want me dead
An uphill battle
Surrounded by a plethora of hopelessness,
An endless supply of depression, alcoholism, self-pity, hypomania,
and self-destruction

I am co-occurring
I happen simultaneously, all at once

God provides me with resources to help me cope with my afflictions
God sends me people to show me how to love myself
God keeps me alive so that I *can* occur and do His will
God saves me so that I *can* happen and be available to others, all at once

~61 days sober

Some-times, Some-things

Lord,

I'm offering myself to You so that You can build me, mold me, and do with me as You see fit. Please, dear God, please "relieve me of the bondage of self" so that I will be capable of doing Your will. Please do me the honor of taking away my difficulties. When we are victorious over them, it will bear witness to those whom I may help of Your amazing power, love, and way of life.[28]

There are some-things that happen some-times where I get stuck. Where I say the words, "I surrender." Where I tell You I am offering myself to You, but there is this darkness inside of me. This darkness that will not detach upon instruction to do so and seek You. It clings to me and corrupts my mood, my perceptions, and my well-being. I am not trying to sound like a helpless victim as I am trying to describe the phenomenon that takes place. I am explaining how I get stuck between talk and action.

Most days I feel I am surrendered. Even on days when things are not happening how I'd prefer them to happen, I pray to You and I practice my new way of life. But then some-times with some-things, I say the same words, I take the same actions, and I can physically feel the darkness inside of me resisting capitulation. I have learned on days like these that greater action is needed. And, sometimes I take it. When I do, relief is not guaranteed but is sometimes granted.

These past few days have truly been a test to see whether I will continue to act or give up because relief has only been granted on a small scale, if at all. I think I should mention again how my darkness can skew my perception. But I will prevail. How can I not with You on my side? Action must continue to be taken, so action I will continue to take.

28. *Alcoholics Anonymous (4ʰ ed.)—"The Big Book"* (2017). Author's personal paraphrase of Step 3 prayer on p. 63.

I ask that You have all of me. Good and bad. I am willing. Remove these defects of mine so that I may be of more use to You and to my fellows. Grant me strength, my dear God, as I go from here to do Your work.[29]

I love You.

Amen.

~63 days sober

Day 67: Take Two

Interrupted sleep
Anxiety about the day?
Reduction in sleep meds?
Regardless the reason
The day is here
Day 67,
We meet again.

My God and I are going to defeat you. You are just twenty-four hours made up of sixty seconds at a time. I have survived the cravings and obsessions of the past relapse. I have stabilized my arrythmias. My body has lost its bloat. My esophagus is no longer burning. My appetite craves clean, healthy food (mostly). I still have "stinkin' thinkin'" sometimes, but it hasn't led me to the bottle. And in that lies victory. Thanking God and my sponsor.

~67 days sober

Havoc

What havoc has my disease created? Havoc amongst those I love? I'd like to say none because I was like the elusive raccoon . . . only coming out at night, separated from others, creating havoc in my own life—not yours, not in my loved ones' lives. I separated myself from others so that I *wouldn't* hurt others. So that I would *only* hurt myself.

But others I did hurt. My isolation and avoidance hurt them. They loved me. They wanted to spend time with me. But I chose

---

29. *Alcoholics Anonymous (4th ed.)—"The Big Book"* (2017). Author's personal paraphrase of Step 4 prayer on p. 76.

to withdraw, isolate, refuse, and decline invite after invite. Pain was caused. Havoc may not have been wreaked, but pain was caused.

Meeting quote: "Your sobriety will never outlive your memory."

~70 days sober

Alcoholics Anonymous

In summary, Alcoholics Anonymous does not guarantee anything if I don't work the steps. Secondly, A.A. adherence doesn't mean my life is going to be amazing. Rather, it gives me the tools that I need. It teaches me how to have reliance on God and how to manage my life without alcohol—both when my life is amazing and when it is the opposite of amazing.

~71 days sober

MY JOURNEY TO RECOVERY

RENEWING THE MIND

The Realization

Trauma. PTSD. *Me? Really?*

Well, my life was threatened by someone at the same time I was struggling with my drinking. Additionally, my now ex-husband was essentially giving me an ultimatum that his existence was based on our relationship status. So I can make sense of how all of that was traumatic. When I received my post-traumatic stress disorder (PTSD) diagnosis, I thought, *This sucks. No one will understand.* At the same time, I thought, *What a relief! Trauma! Thank goodness. That's why I can't seem to control my drinking.* The more I sat with it, the more sense it made. My isolation, my drinking, my cutting, my depression, my anxiety, my anger, my intrusive thoughts, my suicidal thoughts, and my avoidance of certain people/places/things . . . they were trauma symptoms!

Not only was I concerned about my alcohol intake, I was concerned about *my need to have some type of substance at all times.* I kept drinking to the point of having hangovers, and it was *so* hard to wake up in the mornings. I had a genius idea: *I won't decrease my drinking, but I will start drinking coffee too!* Coffee had caffeine. I had always avoided caffeine out of fear it would hinder my mental health medications, but I was at a point where I could not have cared less. I had coffee in the morning before work, I took coffee in a thermos to work, and then I had alcohol as soon as I got home until bed.

But then I realized, I still had a major gap in my day where I was not intaking something. I tried to stretch out my coffee further by increasing to two thermoses at work. I drank two to three cups of coffee in the morning, and then I brought two to three additional thermoses to work. That still only got me to lunch.

Some days, when I really did not care about saving money, or life in general, I would walk to the gas station next to the office and get a big coffee to last me a large chunk of the afternoon. After that, my anticipation of alcohol when I got home carried me through the remaining workday.

Management of this coffee routine became a struggle, so I began brewing my own tea. I started carrying both a lunch bag and a beverage bag into work in the mornings. I would have my two thermoses for my coffee for the mornings and then I would have two large bottles full of caffeinated tea to drink in the afternoons. This was behavior I felt powerless to change. I thought and felt that *I had to have it, I had to do it, I had to be intaking something.* This behavior scared me.

I started receiving counseling in March, but I decided to switch counselors in August of that year. I made the switch because I knew I needed something more than what I was getting from my counselor at the time, and because my suicidal thoughts and alcohol intake were not being taken seriously enough. I told my new counselor, X, that I could count on one hand the amount of days in the previous 365 that I had not had alcohol. I told her I did not know why I couldn't *not* drink. I told her I always had to be ingesting something, and that I did not know why. I told X I had suicidal thoughts briefly in June and that they had just returned. I told her I would sometimes drink, look at pictures of my niece, cry, and say, "I'm sorry," over and over to her because I did not know if Blakely was going to know her Auntie J when she grew up. Or, I did not know what version of J she would know when she grew up. I told X of my amazing support network and how I isolated and withdrew from it. I shared how discouraged I was from helping myself anymore but that I knew I needed help, and that was why I was there.

I should also mention, in the fall of that year, I was at a point where alcohol was affecting me physically. After some blackouts or heavy drinking episodes, I would notice my tremors—where my hands shook—the next several days. My hands would stop shaking once I got home after work and put alcohol in my body again. Then, I would notice the tremors again the next morning when I awoke. My gums became super sensitive and tender, and I kept trying to convince myself it was because I was suddenly brushing my teeth too hard. My teeth became stained (I've since used a whitener kit). I avoided check-ups with the dentist, general physician, gynecologist, and optometrist out of fear they would see me for what I really was and the damage I was doing to myself. This damage . . . this self-destruction that I was aware of but felt incapable of stopping because I did not fully understand it. So what was the point of going to the doctor if I was just going to continue my path of self-destruction?

Speaking of symptoms of self-destruction . . . oh, the heartburn! My heartburn was pure fire. I would go through periods of time where simply putting vodka in my mouth—not even drinking it yet—

meant I would have heartburn for days. During those times, I was prepared. I would simply switch back to wine until the symptoms settled. White wine. Cold, white wine. Not red. Red wine also contributed to fire-like heartburn. I did not mind switching to white wine, except for the financial drain and the physical bloat that lasted for days. It became impossible to maintain my weight. My body temperature was irregular. I even had a coworker once tell me I smelled like alcohol at work. I was mortified. I was losing all control.

Over the next several months, my drinking was addressed in counseling. Too much so, I thought. Whenever I drank, my counselor, X, would want to know what type of alcoholic drink, how much did I drink, for how long did I drink, blah, blah, blah. I thought we figured out my drinking was a symptom of my trauma, and once I kept doing the work to get healthier mentally and emotionally, the drinking would subside into a healthy/moderate balance. But with the way X would question me, it would make me think that *she* thought *I* had a drinking problem! That annoyed me. I just wanted to figure out *why* I was drinking the way I was and *how* to set boundaries. I would go a week here and there without drinking to prove to her I did not have a drinking problem. I once even went three weeks. But then the holidays came.

I celebrated Thanksgiving with my family and managed my drinking in front of everyone, as usual, until I got home and was able to drink how I really wanted. Then, December came. December was horribly stressful at work. I was so stressed even my body suffered and I ended up in the ER! My favorite coping skill? Alcohol. I managed the first half of the month fairly well but the second half, not so much. I was already on a reduced FMLA working schedule to accommodate my PTSD treatment. Then my work schedule was reduced even further with paid holidays with Christmas and New Years. I ended up only working two or three days of the last two weeks of December.

Once Christmas passed, I was in some of the worst mental and emotional pain that I have ever experienced. I did nothing but lie around and drink alcohol. I went days without showering. I had friends that were insistent on spending time with me. I manipulated these plans with friends to occur at my house so I wouldn't have to worry about sobering up or taking a shower. I also planned for them to come over on the same day at separate times so I could get it over with. While they were over, I tried hard to not get too close to them in fear I smelled from my days of gluttony and disregard for personal hygiene. The first friend that came over didn't drink, so I drank before she got there and stole swigs of wine whenever she went to the bathroom. After the first friend left, I drank a little more and took a nap before friend number two's arrival. With friend number two, I was able to openly drink wine with her during the visit. I think I remember most of the visit, but I am not sure. When she left, I drank to oblivion, and my next memory is waking up on the couch with the kitchen and living room lights on, the TV on, and the dogs scattered on the couch sleeping. *Success,* I thought. I made it through the day.

Days later, New Year's Day came along and with it, hope. I felt like I got my drinking out of my system. I finally showered. I saw my sister-in-law, my niece, and my nephew. I thought God was showing me the path to my new world, one where I did not crave alcohol and I could be a part of my family. The next healthy thing to do was turn in my two weeks' notice at work—it was a toxic environment. I was talking to my new boss about working in a healthier environment in a private practice. A private practice! Something I had wanted since I was sixteen years old. Things were turning a corner. Little did I know it would only last a couple of days.

It wasn't long before I again began drinking every night, *but not like I did in December*—I felt that made a difference. The week of January 12th was one I thought would be of celebration, leaving my old job. Instead, it was filled with fear. My last day at work was Thursday, January 11th. My plan for the following day, Friday, January 12th, was to pack up my office, turn in my work laptop, and then celebrate . . . by myself. I have never been against a party of one. My plan for the upcoming day was to blast music, work on my puzzle, drink, eat tasty food, watch funny TV, and do whatever I wanted. Yet, as my last week of work began, as Monday passed, as Tuesday did the same . . . my anxiety and feelings of fear continually increased. Whenever I thought about Friday and "celebrating," tears came to my eyes. I couldn't understand it intellectually. I could only feel it. I could only feel fear. I'd later come to learn in the A.A. program that this is the feeling of powerlessness.

I remember talking to a friend from work with my eyes watering, telling her that I did not want to drink on Friday, but I *felt like I had to.* She tried to be helpful and said we could make plans so I either did not have to drink or I did not have to be alone. With my eyes continuing to water, I just shook my head. I felt complete helplessness about what was going to happen on Friday. I knew I was going to drink to oblivion. Through the previous twenty-seven years of my life, I knew that something could always be done about anything I was feeling or whatever situation I was in. But this, this feeling of fear and powerlessness, is one that is difficult to put into words. It truly felt like nothing could have been done. Nothing could have stopped what was coming.

On January 12th, at approximately 6:40 a.m., I was driving to my office for the last time to pick up my stuff. All of a sudden, as quickly as an exhale changes into an inhale, I had a suicidal thought and a desire to run my car into another. I was traveling roughly 70–75 mph. Realistically, I do not know if death would have been the result, but my brain was telling me to kill myself. Actually, my whole body was. I felt adrenaline. Panicking, I gripped the steering wheel and focused on staying in the parameters of my lane because it felt as though my life depended on it. I was fighting myself. I did not know what was happening. I glanced at my fitness tracker and my heartrate was beating twenty beats higher than usual. I could feel the dilation in my eyes and my heart felt like it was about to beat out of my chest—all signs of the inner battle that was occurring.

Small suicidal thoughts were not necessarily uncommon up until this point. For example, a client baked me carrot cake muffins as a goodbye gift earlier in the week, and I had the thought of eating all of them because *just maybe* it would kill me (carrot allergy). If I was dead, I would not have to battle alcohol anymore. I discarded the muffins because of what they symbolized, and the thought stopped there. These past thoughts had been nothing like what I was experiencing that morning. In this moment, I just focused on the lane and the lyrics of the song that was playing until that moment passed.

Once I made it through fighting for my life, which I had mixed feelings about, and once I finished all my job stuff the morning of the 12th, I stopped by Goodwill and donated my wedding dress. Talk about anti-climactic! Walmart was right next door. *Let's just look at the wine section. OK, maybe it won't be so bad to drink. I deserve to celebrate. I'm finally done with this job! And I'm done with trying to sell that dress!* I bought tasty junk food and lots of wine—the equivalent of ten 750 ml bottles. I wanted to be sure I wasn't going to run out.

When I got home, I had a blast! I immediately started drinking. I blasted music, did some chores, texted friends, worked on my puzzle. I simply enjoyed my time. My friend still wanted to get together with me, but I told her no. This "fun time" lasted for about two hours before I blacked out. Two and a half hours after that, I woke up face-down in my bed, music still playing on my downstairs TV, someone knocking *and* ringing my doorbell, my dogs going crazy because of that, and my cell phone ringing and vibrating. I was in utter confusion. I answered the phone while being unsure of who was on the other line. It was a brief discussion. Someone was still at my door. Hazy, confused, dizzy, I made my way down the stairs.

I answered the door. Apparently, during my blackout I told my friend from work to come over. She was frantic.

"Finally! Where have you been? You tell me your suicidal thoughts this morning while you were driving, and then you make me wait thirty minutes out here, calling you and ringing your doorbell!?"

Disoriented and trying hard to understand what she was saying and why she was at my house, I asked, "What day is it?" I try to understand further. "What time is it?"

She responds, still overwhelmed, "*What?!* Why didn't you answer your door? It's Friday! I just saw you this morning!"

Still trying to understand, I repeated my questions and then told her to come inside. I took her upstairs to show her where I was to maybe help both of us understand what had happened. Upon seeing my bed, things started to make sense. My sheets were half changed. I must've started to change them and either passed out or "closed my eyes for a couple of minutes." My friend shared how frightened she was that I had hurt myself since she could hear the music and saw lights on, but I wasn't answering the door. I started to come to, attempted to apologize, and told her we could still have a good night.

My friend had brought food for us to eat while we watched TV. I was able to pour more wine in a non-wine glass to disguise my drinking. She had no idea I continued to drink the next couple of hours while she was there. However, she figured it out by the end of the night. It was probably due to my slurred speech, glassy eyes, lack of coordination, or my spontaneous idea to paint on my wall upstairs. Before leaving, she poured out the wine in my glass and filled it with water. I was tired and went to bed.

The next day, I tried to piece together memories of what had happened the day before. I swore to myself I wasn't going to drink the wine I had left over in the fridge. Certainly not after the panic and the fear I caused my friend over stupid alcohol. I waited well into the afternoon until I couldn't resist any longer. I felt disgusted as I drank it. Why couldn't I stop? My life was improving! I was out of one job and about to start another! I was about to go on a vacation! Things were getting better! Why was I doing this with my life?!

Then Sunday came, and I attended a therapy session I already had scheduled. I talked to my X about how my drinking over the past month had been getting out of control. She iterated the need for additional support, like when I attended group therapy for trauma in the fall. When she validated my concern about my increased alcohol intake and my powerlessness with alcohol, it made me take a step back. I did not want alcohol to be the problem. Alcohol had become my solution to everything. Part of me knew she was right. However, part of me felt like no real damage had been done on Friday and that I just needed to be extra careful with my drinking in the future. The last thing in the world I wanted to do was give up alcohol. It had become my best friend, even though it was destroying me. I went home and thought things over for hours. I was restless. I paced and paced.

I did not want extra support. I did not want this. I did not want whatever it was all the signs were pointing towards. I just thought and thought and thought. My life had been getting better! I only had a bad weekend. Then again, I thought of a time that I took shots before my best friend came to visit me and how I was sure to drink during and after her visit. I thought of times a friend would ask me if it was OK if they invited other friends to hang out, and the first question I would ask them was, "Do they drink?" I thought of how I'd use alcohol as a motivator. Such as, I would make a drink and then do chores. I could not for the life of me get myself to work out. I motivated myself by working out at home and drinking while I did so. I hated cooking so I drank while I cooked. If I had to catch up on some work at home, might as well be sipping on something while I do it. I got honest with myself and realized that for me to be willing to do anything, I had to have some type of alcohol. After hours of deliberation, I knew what I had to do. My mom and I were leaving in a few days to go on a girl's trip as a celebration for me leaving one job and starting my new one.

My mom and I have many great memories together, and some of them are when alcohol was present. They aren't of us getting wasted together. These memories were not dependent on alcohol. It has just us having a drink while we went to dinner or while we played a game or when we went to see a show. We never needed alcohol to have fun. It was just an additional component that was added after my early twenties.

Thinking of the vacation, I texted my mom to ask if we could have an alcohol-free vacation. Still, to this day, it is the lamest text I have ever written due to how much love and adoration I had developed for alcohol. Then, I investigated additional support to help me. I was ready to admit I had a problem with alcohol. I reflected on my substance abuse course in grad school and how it was mandated to attend two Alcoholics Anonymous meetings. I cringed at the irony and searched local A.A. meetings. There was one just down the road, starting in a few hours.

On January 14th, I attended my first meeting and I started my journey in Alcoholics Anonymous. The journey has been arduous thus far but completely worth it. I've relapsed twice but have been sober a couple of months now. I do believe I was always meant to end up here at some point in my life. I have the genetics for it on the Whalen side, and then being bipolar put me at an even higher risk.

Alcoholism is a progressive disease. I think the stress from my marriage and divorce may have exacerbated the development of the disease. Ultimately, I see it as a blessing that I can work on this now at twenty-eight rather than at thirty-eight or forty-eight years old. Sometimes, people do not make it into the rooms of A.A. until their sixties. I am grateful God helped me realize this when He did. Now, I will continue to work the program by admitting my powerlessness over alcohol and surrendering to God, taking life one day at a time. I am sober.

~72 days sober

God Is My Provider

God is my provider, in all respects. My sponsor, P, has reminded me multiple times that God is my provider, even financially. When I gratefully inherited two thousand dollars recently, my plan was to use it towards my mortgage payments. However, clients are not in school and do not need to be seen as often. The past couple of weeks at the restaurant have been slower, so my income has been affected. I was in a situation of not having enough money to cover both my car payment and my car insurance payment that are due today. I felt so discouraged that I did not have the money from my own earning.

Then, I remembered the extra money I inherited. I deposited the money so my bills would be paid. I prayed to God to change my attitude from discouragement to that of gratitude. God created the situations so that I would have the money today. I am so grateful for that. I need to stay in today. I will take the right actions. God will provide and will help me figure out how to pay my mortgage when that is due in a couple of weeks. His is a plan different than the one I intended, and that is OK. May Thy will be done, *always*.[30] God is my provider. May my heart remain grateful and willing.

~75 days sober

Temporary Sponsor

I love how today's Daily Reflection calls alcohol my "enemy-friend" as well as differentiates the disease from my "moral fiber."[31] When I first attended A.A., I was scared and shy. But I also had some underlying confidence that I was where I needed to be. Someone, who turned out to be my temporary sponsor, initiated conversation with me and even called me later that night, after the first meeting. The counseling world I come from does not work that way. The counselor normally does not call the client. The client has to initiate phone calls, sessions, etcetera. She encouraged me to attend the 10 a.m. meeting the next day where I unknowingly met my current sponsor, P.

Switching sponsors was scary, as I still did not know what the heck I was doing. But I had to follow my heart. I was so concerned about hurting my temporary sponsor's feelings that I did not at the time—or I was not able to until this point in sobriety—see the *small but mighty role* she played in my sobriety. Was it God putting her in my life, briefly, to have interactions over a few days that helped build my

---

30. *Alcoholics Anonymous (4th ed.)*—"*The Big Book*" (2017). Part of the Step 3 prayer on p. 63.
31. *Daily Reflections* (2016), p. 179.

foundation that has helped me stick around for five months and have 75 days sober? Of course it was. I am grateful for God, my temporary sponsor, my current sponsor, and 76 days sober.

~76 days sober

Drop the Rock Reflection

Defects of character are our best attempts to get our needs met. They have saved our lives."[32]

- What purpose or need has any of my self-destructive behavior been serving?
- The hole in my life—not knowing it was there or how to fill it. So I distracted myself with feeding my disease.
- I wasn't bad, just wrong.
- My needs still weren't met, so I repeated the same harmful behaviors.

~76 days sober

Resentment Reflection: Part I

My ex-in-laws did the best they could raising my ex-husband. I have been struggling with resenting the pain their defects caused me, my ex, and our marriage. In this moment, while listening to an A.A. speaker who stated, "They did the best they could," it clicked. In this moment, I still feel some hardness in my heart, but I also feel some peace and some forgiveness. His parents did the best they could.

My ex-mother-in-law (ex-MIL) had a very strict childhood and wanted the opposite for her children. Her eldest child turned into a self-sufficient machine. But for my ex, it only enabled him to be helpless and unaccounted for.

My ex-MIL has a long history of depression but not anxiety. My ex had one of the worst cases of untreated generalized anxiety disorder (GAD) that I have ever seen. I know his mom tried to get him the help he desperately needed, but she was not able to handle his resistance to treatment—and it is a skill she never acquired. Instead, she coddled him. She was afraid to push him too far. She knew more was needed but did not know how to help him.

32. *Drop the Rock* (2nd ed.) by Bill P. Todd W. Sara S. (2005) This is a quote from the last paragraph on p. 5..

My own parents did not know how to handle my mental health struggles, but I was blessed with resourceful, determined parents. My parents did not want me to have a divorce and suffer emotionally, and his did not either. I've maintained anger and resentment because of my ex-MIL's own experience with mental illness and because she could have done more to help him (in my opinion). Our failed marriage put aside, he would just be a happier and healthier person had he gotten more help from the beginning. There was so much potential and so many opportunities available for him when he was young . . . maybe she just couldn't figure out what was best? Or, maybe she did try, and this was her best.

If confronted, she would deny my ex was ever emotionally abusive and manipulative to me, just like she played off her husband's threat to my life. But if she understood the situation in another way, I know she would be mortified by some of her son's behavior. She would not have wanted to raise a son to be that kind of man or husband.

Of course, I had my own role in everything. I'm not trying to play the victim, but I think this might be the start of me finding forgiveness and releasing my resentment towards my ex-in-laws and my ex-husband.

Thank You, God, for this insight. Please help me continue this path of discovering and discarding.

~76 days sober

Resentment Reflection: Part II

What about me? Did I do the best I could through my own spiritual sickness? How my ex and I even ended up married is an entirely different conversation. Right now, I'm focusing on the marriage. Did I do the best I could like I'm saying maybe my ex-MIL did?

The reason the short marriage lasted as long as it did was because I *was* trying my best. I was trying *everything* I knew to do. Whether it was supporting, confronting, encouraging, avoiding, enabling, motivating, crying, begging, moving, couples counseling, separating, praying—anything and everything. I tried to keep our marriage issues between us. I did not share with family and friends until near the end. My coping skills were exercise, my pets, drinking (not yet out of control, but it was increasing), counseling, and psychiatry.

Even though I did not want to be married anymore, I still took actions because I made the decision to marry.

I most definitely did not do everything perfectly. I had my times, too, where I was manipulative, where I didn't let things go, where I wasn't the bigger person, where I wasn't flexible or warm or loving towards my husband. I played a role, too, in the marriage failing. At the time, with where I was and who I was, I believe I tried the best I could. We just were not meant to work.

One of the hardest decisions I have ever made was divorcing my ex-husband. I was out of love and full of resentment and disgust. But I had made a commitment to him, and he was in a time of need. I had a mantra at the time with God: "With You, I'll carry through." I knew I had done all that I could, and both of us were only suffering. I had to end it, and I knew God would carry me through. And He has. He's carried me on a path very different than I anticipated . . . as I'm currently sitting in a room of Alcoholics Anonymous writing this.

What about my ex? Did he do the best he could? Can I find forgiveness? Can I let go of this resentment towards him with the insight and understanding of "he did the best he could"?

~77 days sober

Resentment Reflection: Part III

One of the biggest blocks with releasing my resentment towards my ex-husband is his own admittance of intentionally being cruel. I know I was not always the kindest, I did manipulate to get out of sex, and I could be selfish.

However, my motives were never vengeful or cruel; they were not intended to cause harm. I see now that the side effects of my actions caused him emotional harm, while the purpose was to provide me with relief, isolation, or validation. His intentions appeared to be, as he would say, "Now *you know* how that feels." I wonder, did his being codependent nullify his awareness of being abusive?

Another part of my resentment is that he resented his parents for treating him the way they did, but then he would turn around and treat me the same way.

~78 days sober

Winning Back a Used Me

I have been thinking of recovery from active addiction as *winning back a used me.* This phrase has been resonating with me this week as I have been cleaning my grandmother's old wooden furniture. This furniture has essentially been abandoned in her home for two years while she has lived in a nursing home in Mississippi.

Recently, both she and her belongings have relocated to Georgia, and my garage has been the temporary home of her wooden furniture. Rather, a temporary home and cleaning zone. I've researched online how wood is and should be treated like a living, breathing object. Step by step I've worked with the furniture to clean it properly without causing damage. Just like I've been working the 12 steps in my recovery.

This furniture was exposed to cigarette smoke for fifty years before sitting in stale, stagnant air for the past two years. Thus, the first step for the furniture was to let it air out and breathe some fresh, moving air. Second, I dusted the furniture. Third, I researched how to best clean and polish the wood, and I bought the supplies. Fourth, I cleaned and polished. Fifth, I wiped out the drawers with cleaner. That is the step I just completed.

Sixth, I am going to vacuum inside the furniture for what has fallen in between the drawers throughout the years. Seventh, I am going to put the pieces back together. This furniture is already in better shape than it has been in years. So "winning back" something already used might not be a negative thing—the way I might have interpreted this phrase earlier on in my sobriety.

Having already been used, damaged, broken, and desperate, I have knowledge of what I am working against. Also, I am able to find the passion and motivation to clean, dust, and polish my used self with care and intention on my recovery journey. The truth of it is, God's will and God's work is what is doing the refurbishing in me, but I still must suit up and show up with a willing attitude to do what work is needed.

~78 days sober

Resentment Reflection: Part IV

After talking with my lovely X and P, the messages I received were, "He is a child of God," "He is/was spiritually sick . . . just as I am/was," and, "He was reacting how he knew to react—like a reflex."

I begged my ex and tried to say in the most direct and understandable terms that our marriage was dying. Still, he could not hear me. I now remember that our marriage counselor, at that time, told me that she did not think he was understanding what our problems were . . . almost like he physically/mentally was incapable of comprehending what was at stake, what the problem was, and how to fix it.

This validates things now, but at the time it caused only confusion. How well he acted and how gullible I was to believe that he had understood our problems and our progressions in the past several years of our relationship. It was a lot to comprehend then, and now I have circled back around. He simply was not capable.

He was raised in a malicious home. During our marriage, when he was uncomfortable, stressed, or threatened, he reacted how he was raised to react—which was to retreat or to be malicious. I thought him relaxing and being comfortable to be who he really was, was one of the keys to us being happy together. In reality, it was a key to finding the truth about him, a child of God—yet spiritually sick, emotionally limited, cognitively limited, maliciously reactive, internally tortured person who did the best he could. He tried to turn our married life into his dysfunctional nuclear life. He wanted me to be his mom, but I reminded him most of his dad. We had so much going against us that we could not survive it. Forgiveness I must find and maintain.

~79 days sober

Resentment Reflection: Part V

As I sat in A.A. this morning, I witnessed two people pick up white chips. One person was someone I had never met before. His eyes were tearful as he picked up his white chip of hope. The other was a gentleman I have seen often in my 7 a.m. meetings. A month or two ago, I remember him sharing his story of his relapse when he was weeks away from his one-year-sober birthday. He shared at that time his embarrassment, his guilt, and his shame. I have seen him in meetings since. But today, this morning, he picked up another white chip. My heart breaks for him, and I admire him at the same time. The amount of courage I witnessed from the newcomer and the existing member . . . it is almost like I could feel it myself.

I realized my ex-husband would have never been capable of this kind of courage. It required courage to face our problems. He did not have any—or at least not what was required to save us. Someone cannot give away what they do not possess. I overestimated what he was capable of, and I was in denial of some deficits—in both him and me. However, when I realized the truth and the depths of his deficiencies, I was at a loss. I had never realized the truth before that. I knew we would not make it through life together.

I must release myself from believing he was capable of more. I must allow myself forgiveness to untie myself from the resentment I have towards both the person who was and was not my ex-husband.

~80 days sober

Day 80

Day 80! I have made it 80 days without alcohol. Wow. Thank You, Lord! Thank you, my sponsor. Thank you, my family! Thank you, my new alcoholic friends! Eighty freaking days. Wow!

God is everything. The more I follow a routine, the more I rely on His will (not mine), the more I believe in a power greater than myself to be stronger than my disease, my defects, and my shortcomings, the more I go with the flow, and the more I will find peace within myself and within my God.

~80 days sober

Demi

Yesterday I learned of pop star Demi Lovato's relapse. It has hit me in different ways. She's been an influence in my life since 2011. It was when she was leaving her Disney days behind her and had just left treatment for bipolar disorder, bulimia, self-harm, and addiction. She had released a song called "Skyscraper" that beautifully described my own struggles with mental illness and my motivation to be healthy.

In that same year, months later, I was hospitalized. While inpatient, I could hear the radio the cooks had on during lunch one day, and one of Demi's songs played. I took it as a sign from God that things would be OK. I have even since painted skyscrapers on my wall as motivation after my divorce.

When I learned of my alcoholism, I admired Demi more because of what she does for her physical, emotional, mental, and sober health. I don't agree with everything she says or does, but I definitely respect her.

Today in A.A., we read the foreword of the 12 steps. We discussed its humble beginnings of two men meeting in 1935 and the fact that "in 2017, over two million people have recovered through A.A."[33] I shared how others have influenced my sobriety, but they cannot be the reason I stay sober. I am in my program for me. I am learning tools and truths in A.A. that are undeniable. I shared how I once heard in A.A. that "alcohol doesn't taste as good once you have A.A. in your body." That is true. I shared how my last relapse was awful, and I do not want to go back to that. From what I had learned, I knew exactly what to do after I relapsed and was ready to get help. As much as anyone can inspire or influence me to be sober, it is up to me to be sober and stay sober.

~83 days sober

The True Victor

The disease lurks in the dark
The disease takes control through suggestion and invitation
Before long,
The disease runs the show
The disease inspires cyclical, sinister thoughts
The disease favors negative emotions
The disease controls all focus
The disease has the power
The disease is the power

The human is discouraged
The human is worn out, exhausted

---

33. *Twelve Steps and Twelve Traditions* (2017), p. 15.

The human is beat up, inside and out
The human listens to the lies of the disease
The human confuses the disease's power with his or her own
The human is lost

The Higher Power sees the power of the disease over the human
The Higher Power offers Himself
The Higher Power provides sanity
The Higher Power gives peace
The Higher Power takes away the power of the disease

It is not too late for the human
The Higher Power is in control, if the human allows it
The Higher Power is the true Victor
The human is the beneficiary
The human and the disease equate self-destruction
The human and the Higher Power exist in harmony, peace, and
      serenity

~86 days sober

Learn, Unlearn, Re-learn

I'm grateful to be in this meeting today. Someone shared how he lost his dog nine years ago, and it led to a big drinking binge. He shared he has since gotten another dog and that dog was put to sleep on Friday—and he hasn't had a drink. He said that nine years ago, he used his dog's passing as an excuse to stay in self-pity and to drink. Today, he said, "I'm in pain. I'm not in self-pity, but I'm in pain. But I don't have to drink over it today."

I shared how I was meant to be here today to hear this. Frosty's (my dog's) health is declining. Maybe she will live a couple more years, maybe not. I do not know, but the fact remains that I do not have to drink over it. I told him I am going to remember this meeting when the inevitable happens with Frosty.

Today's topic is about self-pity. A personal favorite character defect of mine. Someone shared, "I have to stay out of the self-pity lane because, if I don't, I will drink again." I currently struggle with understanding what self-pity is, what depression is, and what are just temporary feelings that are OK to feel for the time being. I confuse the OK feelings with sulking, and then I get mad, impatient, defensive, or even more sad. It is incredible everything I am having to learn, unlearn, and/or re-learn throughout this process.

~88 days sober

Resentment Reflection: Part VI

Today in the meeting, we started reading the chapter in "The Big Book," "To Wives."[34] It is a weird chapter for me. I do wonder if, and to what extent, my drinking hurt my ex-husband . . . since my drinking got out of control *after* our marriage. It is weird because I feel like I relate to the "wives" and all the crap they put up with, with their alcoholic spouses. This chapter describes him so well. He hardly drank, but when he did, he would binge. I do not believe he was an alcoholic. Thinking about it, I cannot think of anything in his life that he had a healthy relationship with. We were both unhealthy. I must keep my focus on my side of the street.

Looking back, we did not stand a chance. This perspective helps me feel forgiveness for us both. I must remember to shift my focus, if it ever wavers, back to my side of the street.

~89 days sober

Dear Alcohol: Part II

Dear Alcohol,

I'll be honest, I still miss you sometimes. What I know to be lies still feel like truth sometimes. Your power is undeniable. Your power is also infuriating because you're a power that lives off of invitation. I have a choice to make. I'm more aware of that choice now. The choice is: who/what will I invite today? God's power or yours? One power I can touch, see, smell, and feel the effects of immediately. One power is intangible but all-encompassing. But it requires patience, trust, and willingness. Which will I invite today?

~91 days sober

---

34. *Alcoholics Anonymous (4th ed.)*—*"The Big Book"* (2017), p. 104.

90 Days

90 days since my last taste of alcohol. Red chip! God willing, this number will only grow.

~90 days sober

Meeting Reflection

- Visible actions vs. an invisible disease
- No front lobe, all reptilian brain
- Therefore, I must take actions to put myself back in the frontal lobe to override reptilian part of brain.
- "The only defense against the next drink is a power greater than myself" (A.A. member).
- Religion: following/fellowship of someone else's experiences
- Spirituality: fellowship of my own experience

~92 days sober

Conditions

Confusion. Fear. Those are what I felt when I thought the conditions that were driving me to drink actually improved . . . but my drinking worsened. What? Why? I hated alcohol, but, at the same time, I loved it more than anything else in my life. It had become my best friend. It always helped with what emotion I was feeling. It developed to the point that I did not need a reason to hang out with my best friend. Just my bestie and me against the world.

The point came when I realized my best friend didn't have my best interests at heart. My best friend was hurting me. I had a decision to make: give up alcohol (give up my best friend) or give up on myself completely. I harmed myself more than ever before. And I hurt others more than ever before.

The time came, and I decided. I needed a new best friend.

"I had a drink and then a drink had me." —C. S. Lewis

~92 days sober

Prayer I

Lord,

Help me remain focused. Help me continue to prioritize my sobriety. Help me continue to prioritize You over all. I have reached this three-month milestone, and I am very proud of myself. I'm grateful to You for all that You've taught me in the past six months. Lord, please guard me against my thoughts and feelings of "I've got this" and then acting on them—relaxing too much or not maintaining my routine or my involvement with A.A., You, and other alkies.

I've learned on a deeper level that You only want the best for me. You want me to have it so good, but I get in my own way and mess that up sometimes. But it doesn't change Your love for me or Your desire for me to be good and to have it good. Of the three—me, You, and my disease—I'm the only impatient one. Your patience is the strongest, the most resilient. Help me continue to rely on Your will, Your patience, and Your timing. Thy will be done.[35] You are amazing. Thank You for the gift of A.A. I love You.

Amen.

~93 days sober

Opposite of Fear

Is the opposite of fear freedom and joy? Fear of losing what I have, fear of getting what I want. Fear is incredibly convincing.

I have had triggers lately, but they have only had a brief, minimal impact. When I am hot and sweaty at work—which is daily now at the restaurant because it is July in Georgia and because of my uniform—I am not always triggered by people's choice in beverage. But yesterday, I saw someone drinking a vodka and cranberry. Oh, how satisfying those were when I was hot! But no, that is no longer my life. I remind myself of that. Sometimes I just move on, and other times I pray. It depends on how long the thought lingers, I suppose.

I am grateful for my recovery thus far. This morning, I had to complete an online alcohol quiz/certification for my job at the restaurant. It "educated" and then quizzed me on "signs of intoxication." I found

35. *Alcoholics Anonymous (4th ed.)—"The Big Book"* (2017). Part of the Step 3 prayer on p. 63.

humor in the irony of it. The fact that I could complete it, not be triggered, not feel fear, *and* find humor in it . . . that was God. I do experience the opposite of fear sometimes: freedom and joy. Wow. Thank You, God!

Lord, please help me remain invested in my recovery and in my priorities. Now that I have experienced the freedom of the feeling that is joy, help me stay rooted in You. May my thoughts, feelings, values, and will align with Yours. Help my self-will not run riot.[36] Help me remain willing and open-minded. Thank You for everything. I love You. Amen.

~98 days sober

Meeting Reflection

- Purple chip! I'm on my way! I cannot wait for July to end so August 5th can be here—so I can get my purple four-month chip! This might be my excessiveness character defect at play. I want more and more chips! But, of course, they are not collectibles. They are representatives of my new sober life and time spent in it.
- "When we put things in God's hands, it is better than anything I could have planned" (A.A. member).
- Active drinking (addiction) damages the frontal lobe, which makes it more difficult to make wise decisions.
- Worthy of suffering: I shared in the meeting about what I learned from Victor Frankl in "Man's Search for Meaning." I explained how to be "worthy of my suffering" and how it's a route to find meaning and gratitude towards God and not resentment.

~99 days sober

Dear Fear

Dear Fear,

You are a built-in mechanism to help maintain my safety. The brain is specifically wired to assess threats and to trigger the fight-or-flight-or-freeze response. But, fear, you go above and beyond the task you were programmed for. You consume me at times. You do not only hold me back from harm, you hold me back from good—from socializing, from trying something new, from loving myself. How is it that you malfunction in this way?

---

36. *Alcoholics Anonymous (4th ed.)— "The Big Book"* (2017), p. 63.

I have learned, or am learning, to be less concerned with the "why" and just deal with what "is." Fear, you have become so familiar that I don't even notice you're there at times. I have become fearful of losing something I already possess. I have become fearful of getting something I want. Fear, you are wrong. Over and over. My response needs to be one of gratitude, not anxiety, nervousness, or more fear.

Fear, you stand for many things: **F**udge **E**verything **A**nd **R**un; **F**alse **E**vidence **A**ppears **R**eal. These acronyms explain the relationship I've had with you. Now, what I am trying to do or at least the response I am trying to have is: **F**ace **E**verything **A**nd **R**ecover.

The *only* way I can face you *and* recover from you is to continually surrender to God, to give it up to Him. And, to align my will with His. You are a match for me. You have defeated me many times. But God is bigger than you. The more I align with Him, the smaller you get. The more I align myself with you, Fear, my anxiety increases, my will becomes self-centered, I abandon social relationships, and I believe I am less than what I am truly worth. Essentially, when I align with you, **F**alse **E**vidence **A**ppears **R**eal again. You are convincing as heck, but God's love, God's plan, God's will, and God's security feels better emotionally and makes more sense intellectually.

Fear, your days of running the show are becoming infrequent. As I said, you may be a match for me, but you are *no* match for my Higher Power. With Him, I can be free of you and your selfish, deceitful ways. To my God I shall cling more and more. To you, I shall listen less and less.

I know your ways. You are still going to spring up in one disguise or another. But once I recognize you, I will surrender to my Almighty. Just know that. Goodbye for now, and goodbye for the times in the future that I abandon you and cling to God.

~101 days sober

Day 102

Wow! I've been in the program for 183 days. Sober 102 days. I still have moments where it hits me, "I'm an alcoholic. I battle addiction." It is then easy to think of all I am "giving up" instead of what I am "gaining." Refocusing is a must. Thoughts like that take me further away from God when I need to only draw myself closer to Him.

"Seed has started to sprout in new soil, but growth has only begun."[37]

~102 days sober

Grateful for What I Have

Daily Reflection: July 18

"I no longer need God each minute to rescue me from the situations I get myself into by not doing His will."[38]

I haven't experienced desperation in a little while. I think this is because of the effort I've put into being willing to live life by God's will instead of my own. In no way does this mean I don't need God every single minute, because I do. It is just evidence that I am practicing the spiritual part of my recovery program.

~105 days sober

Authenticity

Every step I took into my disease, I was taking a step away from my genuine, authentic self. Another bottle of wine down . . . away goes my integrity. A couple more vodka drinks . . . there goes more important virtues: honesty and honor. Withdraw more from others, skip showers, ignore responsibilities . . . bye-bye empathy, compassion, and morality. I walked into my disease—rather, at times, I *ran* further into the depths and the darkness of my disease. I no longer knew who I was or how to be without alcohol. Authenticity was long gone. Alcohol was what consumed me.

I consulted my disease before making decisions. If I was invited to go somewhere, my first thought and/or question would be, "Will there be alcohol there?" I would ask myself if I should hang out with a particular person, and then I would have the genius idea to invite them to my house so that I could either drink openly in front of them—also I wouldn't have to worry about driving home and I could fully relax—or I could drink inconspicuously.

---

37. *Alcoholics Anonymous (4ᵗʰ ed.)*—*"The Big Book"* (2017), p. 117.
38. *Daily Reflections* (2016), p. 208.

There was no consultation with my Higher Power. I was fully powered by my disease. Not concerned with character building . . . only concerned with where my next drink was coming from. But now, things are changing.

On days I choose to walk in the Spirit, I get closer to my authentic self. The person God created with care and intention. I want to be who my Maker made me to be. The more I pray, the more I feel whole. The more I drank, the more cracked, fragile, and broken I felt. I choose God. I choose authenticity. I choose to walk with Him.

~105 days sober

Meeting Reflection

I do not know if I had false pride or not. Well, when I look at my actions of not calling to God, relying on God, or surrendering to God, they could be interpreted as me being a prideful individual in the realm of faith and God.

I have either learned, realized, or re-learned that I am nothing without Him. I must call upon Him, talk with Him, rely on Him, and surrender to Him daily. It is through this way and only this way that I have any hope of being useful to Him—to walk the path I was meant to walk. It's the only way I can experience true happiness and joy. Glory be to God!

~105 days sober

Resentment Reflection: Part VII

As Adele says, "We gotta let go of all our ghosts. We both know we ain't kids no more."[39] We worked better as kids. Let's not fool ourselves. As adults, we sucked. I took on everything. I was growing. I was trying to build. You weren't ready for adulthood. What I didn't take on, you tried to get your parents to pick up. Then, more and more, I chose to cope by drinking. It isn't your fault; it is my own for having not seen the truth before we wed.

If our relationship didn't expire the way it did, I might not have gotten on this healthy path that I am on. I am grateful for the end

---

39. "Send My Love (To Your New Lover)," by Adele.

result. I am sorry for the ways I failed you. I truly am. I forgive you for the ways you failed me.

~110 days sober

Prayer II

Lord,

Please guide me as I venture into the healing process from my sexual trauma. Protect me from pain that does not need to be felt and morbid reflection[40] that does not need to be thought, and protect me from engaging in unhealthy coping mechanisms that would only elongate my pain. Help me, Father, as I seek to heal. Please help me grow stronger in my relationship with You on this journey. I want to rely on You as I become more vulnerable by the minute! Protect me, Lord. Of course, above all else, may Thy will be done.[41]

This particular trauma is closely related to my alcoholism. I do not want to drink. I do not want to eat excessively. I do not want to self-harm or self-medicate. Please grant me strength to include You on this journey instead of anything I just listed. I believe this trauma is resurfacing at this time because I am now strong enough in my stability, in my sobriety, and in my relationship with You to deal, cope, and heal from this damage retained by my mind and my body. Above everything, may Thy will be done. I love You. In Your name I pray,

Amen.

~115 days sober

4 Months

Gratitude
8 months in
4 months sober
More time put in
More time given
Greater surrender
Clearer perspective
Glory be to God

~120 days sober

---

40. *Alcoholics Anonymous (4th ed.)*—"*The Big Book*" (2017), p. 86.
41. *Alcoholics Anonymous (4th ed.)*—"*The Big Book*" (2017), p. 63.

Meeting Reflection

- "In God's economy, nothing is wasted. Through failure, we learn a lesson in humility which is probably needed, painful though it is."[42]
- "How thankful I am today, to know that *all* my past failures were necessary for me to be where I am now."
  - "When I sought God . . . He shared His treasured gifts."[43]

As I've said, in my journey towards and in adulthood, I have learned some things about myself that I never would have picked. I'm a bipolar, alcoholic divorcee who has gone through years of suffering and financial struggles. Even with all of that and more, I'm finding gratitude in what my past and current struggles are teaching me.

~126 days sober

If Not . . .

Can I feel the emotions within me without altering my state of being?
If not, I will drink again.

Can I practice rigorous honesty[44] with myself and others?
If not, I will drink again.

Can I surrender, give everything—good and bad—to my Higher Power?
If not, I will drink again.

Can my faith be bigger than my greatest fear?
If not, I will drink again.

Can I accept my thoughts as only thoughts and nothing more?
If not, I will drink again.

Am I OK with *where* I am?
If not, I will drink again.

---

42. *As Bill Sees It* (2001), p. 31.
43. *Daily Reflection* (2016), p. 64.
44. *Alcoholics Anonymous (4th ed.)—"The Big Book"* (2017), p. 58.

Am I OK with *who* I am?
If not, I will drink again.

~128 days sober

Rock Bottom

Something beautiful about Alcoholics Anonymous is that regardless of the height of someone's bottom (high bottom or low bottom), it is still rock bottom. Hard, stone-cold, rock. It hurts falling on that. Like, really, really bad. But that is where serious contemplation happens. That's where life-changing, possibly life-saving decisions are made.

Rock bottoms are internal, external, or both. I had pushed everyone in my life away. I was alone. Alone, drinking. What I hear in meetings is that regardless of the type of bottom—internal or external, high or low—we all seem to end up drinking alone. Alone with the disease. Alcoholism = *the great equalizer.*

With this disease, there is recovery. But, recovery requires humility, willingness, and, certainly not last or least, it requires G-O-D.

~129 days sober

Alcoholic Amnesia

A small thought takes root like a seed in soil
"How about a drink?"

The seed blossoms
"One glass . . . one small bottle . . . it won't hurt."

The rooted tree bears fruit
"You can control yourself now."

Just like that . . .
I'm cured

Away goes the memory of suffering
Away goes the time spent convinced I had a problem

Thoughts take off like wildfire
"It won't be bad this time."

"Remember the fun we had?"

Thoughts and feelings of the companionship return
"Look at what you just went through . . . you deserve the solace of a drink."
"Let's celebrate."

Alcoholic Amnesia
Just like the bear of labor pains leave the mind when the baby is
    placed in a mother's arms
What once was killing me now feels like a long-lost best friend
The fully formed amnesiac tree in my brain craves the comfort of
    that friend

But then, I invite God in
The tree begins to rot and recede
God's grace and power restores
The antidote to Alcoholic Amnesia

~141 days sober

Saved from Myself

The need to be saved from myself
. . . from my bondage of self
. . . from the obsession

The need to be saved from myself
The ultimate pride crusher

The need to be saved from myself
Who can do it?

The need to be saved from myself
The ultimate surrender

The need to be saved from myself
Only my Higher Power is qualified

The need to be saved from myself
God, save me

Being saved from myself
A new freedom

Being saved from myself
A new me is born
May Thy will be done[45]

~142 days sober

Help Me

Lord,

Help me stay willing. Help me practice humility. Help me lean into You. Help me cling to You as I ride out these thoughts and emotions. "Of myself I am nothing, the Father doeth the works."[46] I know I am requesting Your help, and that requires me to do my part. May Thy will be done this minute,[47] the next minute, and all the rest of the minutes of this day. Lord, please grant me understanding of Your plans for my life today, and grant me the strength to carry them through. You are all-seeing, all-powerful. Help me cling to truth. I love You.

Amen.

~153 days sober

Transformed

Annnnndddddd . . . done!
Transformed
I'm officially a butterfly
I've shed my caterpillar past

Now what?
Just as I ate alone, preparing for my butterfly future
I now fly about, from place to place, alone

What is the purpose of my new form?
My insides feel the same

---

45. *Alcoholics Anonymous (4ᵗʰ ed.)*—*"The Big Book"* (2017). Part of the Step 3 prayer on p. 63.
46. *Twelve Steps and Twelve Traditions* (2017), p. 75.
47. *Alcoholics Anonymous (4ᵗʰ ed.)*—*"The Big Book"* (2017). Part of the Step 3 prayer on p. 63.

I take a break from flying and rest on a twig
Another butterfly lands beside me

She speaks, "Isn't today beautiful? The sun is shining, the sky is blue,
 a breeze is blowing. Now I can float along the wind and witness
 God's amazing earth."

Annoyed by the positivity
But curious just the same
I ask, "How long have you been a butterfly?" assuming it had been
 for some time
She replies, "For two sunsets and one sunrise."
I think, *Why couldn't she just say two nights and one day?*
I demand, "How are you so happy?"
"Because I'm free. I've shed the constraints of my old life, and now,
 now I can travel and smell and see all of God's creation. There
 is something new every day. Life has such incredible meaning!"

I ask, "But what about purpose? What is our purpose?"
"To be God's beauty. To serve His purpose."
I anxiously inquire, "What is His purpose? How will I know if I'm
 doing His will or my own?"
Calmly, she responds, "You will know."

~159 days sober

Divorcing the Past

It's no longer working
Holding onto you, the past
You continually haunt me, now, in the present

I have to let you go
I no longer need you
You've taught me many lessons
You've taught me right from wrong
And wrong from right

But now, you hold me back
You heighten my expectations
You increase my sensitivities
You expand my insecurities

You limit my interactions
You torture me with a lack of trust in myself and in others

Tired of being lonely
Tired of being held back

It's time I expand my horizons
It's time I move on

I feel lighter
The sun shines brighter
Color is more vibrant
To continue on this journey
I must remain adamant
No turning back to the past
Only forward thinking from here on out
Help me, dear Father—continue to work this all out

~167 days sober

6 Months

G od and I have done it! I am grateful for my God and for our deepened relationship. I am grateful for improved relationships and increased participation with my family. I have since taken a step back from counseling to focus on my sobriety. So, in addition to waitressing, I am grateful to have found a new job where my sobriety is a requisite and for my boss who is also in the program. I am grateful for taking my physical health more seriously and having lost twenty pounds. I am grateful for completing my first doctor's appointment since getting sober and following through for the second visit in the same week. I am grateful to have found my home group, my sober family. I am beyond grateful for my sponsor who talks to me in whichever way I need—soft and gentle, like a firecracker thrusting the truth in my face, like a cheerleader championing my efforts, or as a friend and a fellow servant of God. I am so grateful for my counselor who has been a lighthouse, helping me navigate myself in and through the darkness.

Thank You, Lord, for Your blessings and my ongoing sobriety!

~180 days sober

A Broken Heart

A heart so broken
I can't hold onto all the pieces

As I pick up a fallen piece,
A different one slips through my grip

I give up
I drop everything
I let go of my heart

With empty hands,
Eager to hold
I pick up the bottle

After time spent
I forget about my broken heart . . .
Left on the ground, unprotected

Hesitation
Social isolation
Disbelief
Sunken dreams
Absent desire
Gaps of time go missing
Avoidance

My grip becomes tighter and tighter
Who needs a heart when I have the bottle instead?
It's amazing. It's the best. It's my bestest friend
But I wish more than anything to be dead

My heart, in its broken condition,
Screams to me about the self-abuse
And the way I've been living

Torn between my brokenness and my best friend
I combine the two, trying to make it work 'til the very end

Drunkenly, I stumble to pick up the pieces of my heart
Piece by piece, part by part

My inebriated equilibrium causes me to tumble
Breaking my heart further
I abandon the mission
And drink even harder

Consequences
Unrecognizable decisions
Foreign person staring back in the mirror
Blackouts
Running away from everything I know
Deeper into the abyss I go

Does hell come after death or is it what I'm living?
All alone with the bottle
My life caters to its contents
Willing to risk more and more for its lies and evilness

The bottle lets me down,
It no longer helps me up
Torn down, pulled away
No one can hear me cry

Suffocated
Out of options
Restless
Exhausted
Seeing double
Beat up
Emotionally bruised

God directs me to the rooms of others
God directs me to A.A.
God heals my broken heart
It's all put back together
Like it was at the start

~193 days sober

Living a Life of Envy

Living a life of discontent
Living a life of envy

Why can others drink, and I cannot?
How can others drink, leave some in the glass, and walk away?
There are only a couple of sips left!
Have some respect for the drink!

Who am I to judge?
Who am I to dictate and disagree?

Holidays, game days, birthday celebrations
All are paired with liquor and good times
Subtract the liquor,
Will the good times remain?

The truth is
Whatever remains is God's plan for me
Acceptance is my only choice

Living a life of acceptance
Living a life I was given
Reasons I have not
But answers have been made clear

I can no longer drink like a normal person
I no longer sip, I only gulp
Once I start with the bright light of alcohol and its associated joy,
    laughter, and giddiness
I don't stop until I black out
Until the bright light fades and I'm only left with depression, memory
    gaps, and a hangover
That is not a life I envy

~195 days sober

The Winds

Through conscious contact
Prayer and meditation
God has given me a sixth sense of direction
A sense allowing the ability to be in tune with Him
And His will for me
He helps me understand I cannot control the winds

The winds of fear
The winds of adversity
The winds of conflict
The winds of financial struggles
The winds of emotion
The winds of disconnection
The winds of spiritual bankruptcy

Even though I cannot control the winds
With His almighty grace,
I can adjust my sails

~212 days sober

Potholes

Driving my sober vehicle
Down a road paved with resentments, fears, and insecurities
Dodging potholes of self-pity
Focusing on driving forward
Not fixating on the pain in the rear-view
Only stopping to make an amend
Or to talk to a fellow with a similar driving experience

Back on the road
I've emptied my cup of liquor
But I've replaced it with discontentment and self-doubt
Trying to drive the car without guidance
I drive straight into a pothole of self-pity
I stay stuck, unable to dislodge my car
I sit there
Suffocating in my own self-pity

Feeling like I am at an end
When I'm really at a start
I pray
I reach for help
A fellow helps my car out of the hole
I get out of the car
I get in the passenger side
And, I allow God to drive

~218 days sober

Then vs. Now

Sips vs. Gulps
Memories vs. Blackouts
Hangovers vs. Withdrawal Symptoms

Enter A.A.
Chaos vs. Stillness
Worry vs. Serenity
Self-Will Run Riot[48] vs. Surrender
Obsession vs. Peace
Anxiety vs. Closeness to God

~220 days sober

The Problem, The Solution

Don't care if I'm alive or dead
But no doubt, the truth has been said
Bipolar, alcoholic
Self-seeking, self-centered
Spiritually sick
Emotionally unstable

This is the life I was given
But it is not the life I have to live

Statements I hear
Choices I must make

Self-pity
Or depression?
Both?
Does it matter?

Regardless
I desire my old coping skills
Honestly, just the one
The drink
The bottle
The sauce

---

48. *Alcoholics Anonymous (4ᵗʰ ed.)*—*"The Big Book"* (2017), p. 63.

John Barleycorn

Whatever the name
The vice grip on my life remains
Like submerged in water, desperate for air
Or sinking in quicksand with no one to hear
My cry for help as I stubbornly focus on what I am without

Alcoholism
Mental obsession
Physical allergy
Spiritual emptiness

The delicate balance of sobriety
Mental focus
Physical abstinence
Spiritual surrender and reliance
Full-time commitment
Full-time sobriety

I must be willing to go to any length
Or else my destiny is certain
Death, hospitals, or incarceration

I insist I'm alone, but I am always with
My Higher Power and the peace He brings
The solution is not a myth
It's the truth straight from one of A.A.'s founders Bill W.'s[49] lips

Will I listen?
Will I refute?
Only time will tell

As stated, the truth has been said
Both the problem and the solution

God, help me bring it into fruition

~220 days sober

---

49. Bill Wilson: one of the founding members of AA. A code way to ask someone if they are an alcoholic is to approach them and say, "Are you a friend of Bill's?" So, anyone who is in the program will know. His story is referenced starting on page 1 in *Alcoholics Anonymous (4th ed.)—"The Big Book"* (2017).

Are You Still There?

Dear God,

Are You still there? Do You still know me? Do You still love me? I don't feel You right now, but I'm still talking to You. Waiting. Am I waiting for You to speak or show a sign? Am I waiting for me to recognize Your presence?

I miss our closeness. Me and You vs. the world. For whatever reason, I'm feeling this . . . this disconnection. I know there is a purpose. Because, once I feel us reunited, that is when my peace will return.

In the meantime, I'm wanting to find spiritual fulfillment in the bottle. I know, intellectually, this will strain our relationship further. But, as You know, I feel so intensely, so convincingly, that I'm really struggling to stay sober.

However, if I have learned anything from You, it is that time heals wounds. Patience pays off. This too shall pass. Be still and know. I have also learned from You that You must be everything to me, or else You're nothing to me.[50]

Therefore, you are everywhere. The green light to get to my meeting on time—that was You. The fact that I made it through yesterday, and every day the past seven months without a drink—that was You. You're everything and everywhere. I love You. Grant me strength to continue to see You and live by Your will.

~221 days sober

Yesterday

Yesterday
Yesterday I almost went to the other side
The side of misery
The side of alcohol
The side of lies
Lies of peace
Lies of healing
Lies of excitement
Lies that I am no longer an alcoholic
Yesterday

---

50. *Alcoholics Anonymous (4ᵗʰ ed.)—"The Big Book"* (2017), p. 53.

Yesterday I almost went to the other side
The side of consequences
The side of losing it all
The side of lies
Lies of companionship
Lies of fun
Lies of recapturing my true self
Lies that I can control my drinking
Today
Today I am sitting in a meeting
Today I am showing up
Today I am learning how to surrender, once more, to my Higher
    Power
Yesterday I had pain
Today I have hope
Yesterday I was lost inside of me
Today I am reaching out to God, other alcoholics, and anyone else
    who wants to hear me or wants me to listen
Yesterday I was living in the problem
Today I am living in the solution

~221 days sober

48 Hours Ago

I am extremely grateful to have not had a drink in seven months, seven days, seven hours, nine minutes, and forty-nine seconds. Forty-eight hours ago, I did not think I would be sitting here in a meeting *and* over seven months sober. I thought relapse was certain. I thought it was decided. But here I am, sober. Not twenty-four-hours sober. Not hungover-sober. Not, "Crap-I-have-to-pick-up-another-white-chip" sober. I am sober. Stone-cold, warm-blooded sober. God's love and interventions are very evident when I review the past couple of days.

Two days ago, even after going to a meeting and after being of service—even after talking to my sponsor and after talking to my family—I became consumed by my disease and the "truth" that I *know* is just a lie.

I had one shift to work and then I would have three days off. I had decided to call into work "sick," leaving me with the next three and a half days to drink and do whatever I pleased. I picked up the phone to make the call into work, and in that instance, my phone rang instead. It was my sponsor. How is that *not* God's intervention? My sponsor told me if I really wanted to drink, and if I was going to call out of work, I should go to the 12:15 p.m. meeting *and then* decide to drink or not. "OK," is all I could say.

I then called work and the general manager answered, who herself is a recovering drug addict. I could not lie. I was honest: "I was going to call in sick, but that is a lie. The truth is, I am really struggling, and I really need to go to a meeting." She wanted to give me the time but offered a compromise because three people had already called out. She said I could go to a meeting and then come into work late. I appreciated the compromise, but I decided to go straight into work since I was just down the road and the restaurant was three people down.

God. God was looking out for me. A large party was placed in my section, but the host said management decided it would go to a different server. God told the manager, the manager told the host, and the host told me.

My sponsor was texting me and was encouraging me to talk to other alcoholics because she did not think I was hearing her. *God.* God told P to tell me to reach out to other alcoholics, and He had her do something unusual—she asked some alcoholics to reach out to me! I was able to text with one of these people while I worked.

God helped in yet another way. He put the thought in my head that my counselor was just down the road. *God.* God made an appointment available for me the minute I left work. God gave X the words to get through to me. I acted a fool in session, but I was so emotionally exhausted from my contemplations to relapse that I was fairly certain I could make it home without stopping at the liquor store. I called an alcoholic and my sponsor. I arrived home, took care of my pups, shared with my mom, and then went to bed. Before falling asleep, X called me to encourage me to attend a substance abuse group at her practice the next day free of charge! *God!*

The next day, Sunday, God pushed me to attend two meetings as well as a substance abuse group. From 7 a.m. to 3 p.m., I was either in a group or a meeting or talking to another alcoholic. God made it *all* available. God helped me in every way to make it through the previous forty-eight hours sober.

Now it is Monday. I forgot to set my alarm for the gym, but God had my dad text me at 4:34 to wake me up so I could still work out! Due to our current schedules, my dad and I are able to meet in the mornings to work out together. It's a current gift of my sobriety to have this quality time with him, and it was a gift to not miss out on it this morning. Sitting in my morning meeting . . . I'm feeling OK. I feel fairly confident that I won't drink today. With God's grace, I will make it. Seven months, eight days, nine minutes, and forty-nine seconds sober. I will take on life twenty-four hours at a time. God is good . . . all the time.

~222 days sober

Butterfly Effect

I am the direct result of the founders of Alcoholics Anonymous, Bill W. and Dr. Bob.[51] Early in Bill's sobriety, he was faced with a daunting decision: go into a bar of a hotel where he was staying, have a drink, and relapse, or call another alcoholic in an effort to maintain his fragile, newfound sobriety. Bill chose God and chose sobriety. Story has it that the alcoholic he called was Dr. Bob. Reportedly, Dr. Bob did not want to speak with Bill, but his wife insisted that he did. Dr. Bob obliged, and, down the road, the two of them formed a small group called Alcoholics Anonymous.[52] A small group which now has an estimated membership of two million people and exists in countries all around the world.[53]

What if Bill went into that hotel bar instead of making that phone call? What if Dr. Bob's wife was not insistent about him meeting with Bill? What direction would their lives have gone? Would they ever have gotten sober? If they never got sober, would I be sober right now? Would my sponsor be? What about the others?

I am grateful history has unfolded the way it has and that I do not have to know the "what ifs." I am sober.

~236 days sober

---

51. Dr. Bob's story is referenced starting on p. 171 in *Alcoholics Anonymous (4th ed.)—"The Big Book"* (2017).
52. https://www.hazelden.org/web/public/has00522.page
53. This fact is from the first paragraph (p. xxii) in *Alcoholics Anonymous (4th ed.)—"The Big Book"* (2017).

Big Book Study[54]

- Alcoholism is of the mind and of the ego. It is not about alcohol.
- Ego isn't bad, but an over-inflated ego is.
- Ego is being in touch with the outer world.
- Ego is me thinking about me—positive or negative thoughts.
- Steps 1 & 2 are conclusions.
- Step 3 is a decision.
  - o Working Step 3 is working the rest of the steps.
- Step 4: Not "looking for my part." Rather, looking for my faults or what I've done.
  - o Looking for "my part" implies someone else still has a "part."
  - o Root word for responsibility is *response*.
    - ▪ It goes back to not what my *part* is but what my *fault* is.
- "Surrender" is moving over to the "winning side." It is not something of defeat.

~242 days sober

Changes

I changed the interior of my home, I changed (divorced) my husband, I changed jobs . . . but problems remained because I remained. My drinking changed as well! For worse!

Another change: I came to Alcoholics Anonymous. I learned why I have always felt so out of place, like I couldn't quite fit in. I knew a big reason was because of my darkness—my close associate and, at times, my best friend. Ego, depression, self-pity, and stubbornness were all barriers I maintained for years when it came to personal relationships and overall quality of life.

With God, fellowship, unity, and sponsorship, I have been sober for almost eight months. And I'm raising my hand to sponsor someone else. This is proof more change is happening and that I am changing with it. I am changing my interior and exterior. Man, has it been painful! But it has been beautiful and bountiful. Thanking God and my sponsor!

~243 days sober

---

54. *Alcoholics Anonymous (4ᵗʰ ed.)—"The Big Book"* (2017).

Extra Weight

Like a sprained ankle
I can't help but step on my pain

Breathing in
Breathing out
It hurts just the same

I scratch at the lonely
But it only multiples
Emptiness so intense
It wakes me up at night

I awaken with a tortured soul
Stuck between dusk and dawn

I wallow so much inside myself I slip when I try to step out
I suffocate in my own self-pity
Desperate for reassurance

God speaks . . .

Why scratch? Why claw towards anything but Me?
You're searching for secular means to fulfill your emptiness
Why not search for Divine Fulfilment?

You stay stuck in your world
Believing your options are limited
Why not reach for My world?
My love, My holiness, and My grace are beyond anything of your earth

You choose to carry this extra weight on your own
Don't you remember?
I'm the One more capable of carrying it
Let your guards down
Set the extra weight on the ground

Breathe
Inhale Me
Exhale the pain
Reach for Me
Let you and Me be all that remain

~248 days sober

A Divine Plan

Before my birth, God intervened and sent an angel to my mom's bedside to say, "You will have a girl and she will be OK." Then, as birth came and complications with it, *I was OK.*

Years later, I thought a handful of coins looked appetizing, so I consumed them. I choked on them and someone intervened to clear my airway. *I was OK.*

Since I was a teenager, I have struggled with darkness, depression, and suicidal thoughts. God has, in His way, given me restraint to not take my own life. There have been minutes, hours, days, and months in between the suffering when, as the angel promised, *I was OK.*

More years pass, more afflictions and more pain, but right now, *I am OK.* "Great suffering and great love are A.A.'s disciplinarians; we need no others."[55] I have experienced great pains, and I have experienced love and grace from my Heavenly Father. He has a plan for me. And it has been made clear that that plan includes me staying alive and not taking my own life.

I am a girl, now a woman, always a daughter of God, and *I am OK.*

~260 days sober

Family Christmas Devotion

Some believe God to be resentful and One to hold grudges. I do believe that He never forgets and that there will be judgment. But the God I know is also merciful, and His love for us is relentless. I read a devotion that described God's love for us in this metaphor of owning a puppy. No puppy comes potty trained or trained in any regard. When taking on a puppy, it requires extra patience and extra understanding. When the pup potties in the house, we know the puppy is only doing what a puppy does. When a puppy chews on something they shouldn't, we know they're just being a puppy. Even though we get flustered and disappointed, we forgive the puppy because we still love the puppy.

We are the puppy. God wants us to learn from our mistakes, and He will certainly hold us accountable for our actions. But He also knows

---

55. *As Bill Sees It* (2001), p. 27.

the heart of man is fallible by nature. Just as puppies grow into dogs and learn from their mistakes, we do too. And, just as dogs still make mistakes—falling for temptation, using the bathroom inside, eating something they shouldn't—we still make mistakes. We give into temptation, we speak when we shouldn't, we are gluttonous, envious, slothful, etcetera, etcetera. *But our human nature does not excuse our sins.* God wants us to grow and learn to be better and do better too.

We love a puppy despite it peeing on the rug—and regardless of what we do or don't do, God still loves us. He still forgives us.

God sent His Son so that we could communicate directly to God, so that we could be freed from our sinful ways, and to show us what perfect, non-judgmental, unconditional love looks like. For that, we celebrate this day.

~265 days sober

Family Christmas Prayer

God,

Thank You that we are all here together under one roof. Thank You for being there for us regardless of our flaws. Thank You for supporting us and helping us improve. Whether we are spiritual beings having human experiences or human beings having spiritual experiences, thank You for sending Your Son to show us the way to the Truth and the Light. Help us be more like You and Your Son, whose birth we celebrate today. Thank You for this family and for loving us. We love You. In Jesus' name,

Amen.

~265 days sober

9 Months

9 months! Green! Green chip! We did it, God!

Nine months ago, I was twenty-four hours sober. I had awoken drenched in sweat. I felt shaky all over. I had acid reflux that felt like lava. My head ached. I was pacing around my living room because my heart would not settle. My mind relentlessly raced. I was both hopeless and hopeful. I was determined to not give in again to the monster—the monster of addiction.

Twelve months ago, I was . . . little did I know at the time . . . nine days away from entering the room of Alcoholics Anonymous for the first time.

Now, one year later and nine months sober, my heart has settled and is at peace while resting in God's hands. I have gotten off several medications, and I have decreased dosages in others. I am the most stable that I have been in—well, the most stable I think I have ever been. I have made peace with much of my past. I have made peace with the future and the uncertainty it holds. I now live twenty-four hours at a time. I used to take full-on hiatuses from the present and live in the baggage of the past or the worry of tomorrow. I still have times where I try to live in yesterday or in tomorrow, but that is now only occasional and for brief periods of time.

My financial status is not very different from a year ago. However, my financial insecurities are more secure. That does not mean that I have more money, that I do not care about my finances, or that I have stopped working to improve my situation. Rather, it means I have more trust that God will provide for me. He will put me in the right place at the right time, and I will be financially stable in His time. In the meantime, He has blessed me with the means to still make my ends meet. Honestly, reflecting on my history with money and my past relationship with money, I think God wanted me to work on non-material things first. I have made incredible progress regarding my spiritual health, my sobriety, my mental health, my emotional health, and my physical health (thirty-two pounds gone in the first year of sobriety!).

It is truly amazing. I have no idea which direction my life is headed. I am a fully licensed mental health professional with a master's degree, and I am currently working as a server in a restaurant. Twelve months ago, I would be losing my mind about finding my purpose, not being in my career, blah blah blah. I have wondered what my purpose is, but I now believe it is to follow God and follow the plans He has for me—not the plans I have for myself.

My anger has mostly resolved. The walls of my resentments have been torn down like the Berlin Wall. I am still hyper-sensitive, but I internalize less. I still get depressed, but for not as long. I still get hypo-manic, but it is less frequent. My life contains much more love, peace, serenity, joy, and God than it has in years, and I am so grateful.

I am grateful for my family and my friends, for my sponsor, and for my sober community. And, most importantly, I am so grateful for my Higher Power whom I call God.

~276 days sober

Spiritual Awakening

I once purchased a three-canvas portrait of an elephant walking down a path. The elephant is facing the viewer and is walking away from stormy skies into sunlight. The elephant is alone with worn-out patches on its feet and tattered edges along its ears. One can easily tell the elephant has been through struggles and its own personal battles. I purchased this art because I related to the elephant. I connected with the elephant being alone. I empathized with the wounds of its suffering, feeling they mimicked my own. I championed the elephant for walking out of the darkness and into the light—what I, despite my own battles, aspired to do.

After entering A.A. and working some of the steps, and after many twenty-four-hour days sober, I saw the elephant portrait in a way I never had before. I saw God. God was the elephant. I must have been on the elephant's back, not pictured. God had the worn-down feet and tattered ears. God was the one fighting my battles this whole time. He was carrying me. He never left me and never wants to leave me. He wants to carry me, to love me. God was the elephant *all* along. I was *never* alone.

~278 days sober

Step 12 Reflection

From being "powerless," "spiritually bankrupt," and "not only in conflict with ourselves, but also with people and situations in the world in which [I] lived," to "cleaning house" and relying on "a source of strength which, in one way or another, [I] had hitherto denied [myself]." My Higher Power, my God, continues to help me "remove shortcomings," and, as a result of this and of my following the 12 steps, God has restored me to "sanity."[56]

I have learned I cannot control the past or the future. I can only pray for God's will to be done and that I follow His plan accordingly. Through my spiritual awakening, I have learned He truly desires to

---

56. *Twelve Steps and Twelve Traditions* (2017), pp. 106–109.

carry my burdens for me. My God loves me so much that He wants to share not only my joys but also my pains. Oh, how blessed I am to have grown in my spirituality!

~279 days sober

Focused on Others

My Momo (grandmother) waited for over a year to move to Georgia to be closer to her family—to see her grandchildren for the first time in years and to see her great-grandchildren for the first time ever. However, she is not happy here. She wants more than anything to return to Mississippi. She wants "to go home," even if it is only returning to her previous nursing home and not her actual home. She is getting what she wants, what will make her happy.

The focus needs to not be on myself and whatever hurt feelings I could easily come up with that she is choosing her home state over her own family. The focus is on her, as it should be, and on what makes her happy. I am grateful for the tools I have gained and the progress I have made in my emotional maturity to have this perspective on the situation.

~279 days sober

Prayer III

Lord,

Thank You for loving me. Thank You for accepting the fallible, sinful, more-likely-to-get-it-wrong-than-right human being that I am. Thank You for encouraging me to not resent or judge the other fallible human beings, events, and situations in my life. Instead, You ask that I accept them for what they are, for who they are. Thank You for not asking me for perfection. Rather, You ask that I just try my best. You ask me to do my part in making myself better and in treating others how I would want to be treated. Thank You for allowing me to be human. Thank You for forgiving me when I misstep. Thank You for comforting me when I am down. Thank You for celebrating me when I do right by You and Your will. I love You.

In Your name,

Amen.

~283 days sober

The Great Chicken Confession

My most complicated amendment to date: The Chicken Amendment, also known as The Great Chicken Confession. The story starts with one of my personality strengths (or in A.A. terminology, one of my *character assets*) getting the best of me. In this instance, it was a character defect. I am an opportunistic person. It has brought me many good things in life. However, last week, I sought an opportunity that was ultimately deceitful as it took advantage of trust others have in me.

A server walked to the back line with wings she had just left the kitchen with. She said they were made incorrectly. I asked if I could take them home, but she said she was just going to eat them there. Her table. Her food. I understood. Later, a cook at work offered to make me chicken wings at the end of my shift to take home. This was the moment that I should have said, "Thank you, but no thanks." Instead, I saw an opportunity to get free, delicious food. I felt my eyes get big as I said, "Could you get me pulled chicken instead of wings?"

"Yeah," he responded, "How much do you want? One pound? Five pounds? Ten pounds? White chicken? Dark chicken?"

Surprised at the amount of food he was offering and excited at the opportunity, I eagerly asked, "Can you get me a pound of pulled chicken?"

He said, "Yeah, just let me know when you are leaving."

I went back to work thinking of how many meals I would get out of this free one pound of chicken! Once I let him know when I was leaving, he prepared the meat. He handed it to me and inconspicuously said, "Here is your bread, ma'am." He said this because he put it in a to-go box servers normally give customers bread in to take home.

"Thank you," I responded, and then I walked out of the door with my pound of chicken.

Normally, whenever I buy food, I must ask a manager's permission and then use their card to get my fifty percent discount. Then, once I receive the food, I must show a manager the container to show I was not stealing any extra food than what I purchased. Sometimes I will have to-go containers when I am allowed to take home food that was incorrectly made and could not be sold.

My parents are incredible human beings that taught me right from wrong. I would not have anything I have today without them. My mom specifically is an amazing negotiator, bargain shopper, and opportunist. She did her best to raise me with these particular skills. She taught me to read between the lines; she taught me to see the grey in black and white situations. She influenced me and my perspectives to see how a situation can be made better for myself and for others involved. This helped me develop self-confidence and develop skills of advocacy, whether for myself or for others, since advocacy is a big part of the mental health and substance abuse field.

A day or two after I got my free loot, I was feeling proud that I was offered free wings but upgraded it to a pound of chicken, so I told my mom of my latest feat. To my surprise, she stated, "Jessica, do you not feel guilty about this? This is stealing." Her statement blew my mind. *What?! I just scored free chicken! I was offered free food. I did not go and seek this food.* But, alas. My mom was right. If it wasn't stealing, why did my coworker need to tell me he was giving me bread? Why didn't he just say, "Here is the pound of chicken that you didn't ring up or pay for?" Duh, he didn't say that because we both would have been reprimanded. It was stealing. I had gotten caught up in the moment and lost sight of the morality of the situation for the opportunity of it. Now that I recognized I had done something wrong, I changed my focus on how to make it right . . . how to make amends.

I initially thought a "living amends" of learning from this chicken situation and never doing it again would be amending enough. As Step 9 states, "Make direct amends to such people whenever possible, except when to do so would injure them or others."[57] Since this situation involved more than me—the cook and the fact that my brother works for the same company—it could reflect poorly on them and cause them consequences. My sponsor agreed with the reasons as to not make a direct amends but shared there might still be a way to make amends even if we could not identify it yet. We talked about ways I could pay the restaurant back, such as ringing up a pound of chicken, paying for it, but not actually taking the chicken. We talked about me doing extra chores for the restaurant. Every idea we came up with, there was a reason why it would not work. P asked that I re-read Step 9, pray, and remain willing.

---

57. *Twelve Steps and Twelve Traditions* (2017), p. 83.

After a day or two in reflection, an idea came to mind. My coworker purchases a salad every day before leaving work. The idea was that I pay for her salads until I reach the dollar amount equivalent to one pound of chicken. This way, I was paying restitution by getting money back into the restaurant that I was not benefiting from personally. I felt good about it and my sponsor approved. It seemed to be the solution.

My next shift, I told my coworker of the plan. She told me I was overthinking the situation and that if I do anything, I should make direct amends to the general manager (GM). Puzzled, I thought she would be satisfied with getting a couple of "free" meals. I tried to explain to her how it was bigger than just me confessing because it could cause harm to others, but that an amends still needed to be made. She disagreed and stated she was uncomfortable with me giving her money. Nevertheless, I relentlessly insisted. She took the money and said it would be the only time. I told her that was not the case because I was only paying half of what a pound of chicken cost.

Excited to be halfway done with making restitution, I called my sponsor to give her the details. She pointed out, correctly, that I imposed my self-will on my coworker. My coworker said she was uncomfortable with playing a part in my amends, but I did not listen. Truthfully, I did not much care about her opinion because I wanted this chicken amendment *done*. Again, she asked me to stay in prayer and to stay willing. Frustrated with my sponsor's truth, I agreed.

My brother and I are seldomly in the restaurant at the same time. The day after I forced my coworker to take my money, my brother happened to be there. I thought, *What a sign from God! I had my brother as a resource this entire time, but I did not think of him until God put him right in front of my face.* I confided in my brother. No detail was left out.

He was quiet for a moment before he told me, "Since you are feeling guilty about this, I think if you have a closed-door discussion with the GM and tell her what you told me, in the same way you told me, I think she will handle it well."

I felt excitement and relief. I appreciated the opportunity to seek my brother's advice. I was grateful his advice was to make a direct amends. Off I went to find the GM so I could finally get this off my chest and be done with this freaking amendment.

Naturally, the GM was busy. But as soon as she was available, I was right there to ask if we could speak for a few moments. Sitting in her office with the door closed, I told her the whole story. I started from the incorrectly made wings, to wings becoming chicken, to chicken becoming one pound, to leaving with my "bread." In hindsight, I realized I made a terrible mistake in this amends. I used names. I did not stay on my side of the street. I identified all the parties involved. My sponsor would chew me out for this later.

Regardless, the GM offered understanding. She thanked me for telling her. She even offered to give me free food sometime if I ever needed it. I offered to pay the store back, and I asked if there was anything I could do to make it right. She said there was not, and there was no need to pay it back.

Relieved, I thought this chicken saga was finished. Excitedly, I texted my sponsor that the amendment was done and that I would call her after my shift to give her more details. When I called, I left a voicemail explaining what happened. I admitted to using the cook's name but focused on the fact that I was able to make a direct amends, and, in my opinion, no one else was harmed. I explained it seemed like I just brought the GM's awareness to food being given away instead of purchased and that she did not seem like she was going to condemn the cook.

Later, my phone rang. My sponsor, rightfully so, asked why I went straight from my brother to the GM. She asked why I did not call her or another alcoholic to talk about it. She asked *why* I said the cook's name. I had no other explanation except for getting caught up in the moment. I told her I understood that part was wrong, but I had been feeling like this amends had gone on long enough and passed a point of ridiculousness days ago.

As my sponsor went on, my frustration turned to a deep sadness. I explained how I felt this entire situation had been blown out of proportion and how I thought God had brought me the opportunity in the first place with my brother and the GM being available. She saw the situation differently. She saw how I practiced self-will, yet again—like forcing my coworker to take my money because I just wanted to be done, I wanted to settle my anxiety, I wanted to be done talking and thinking about the stupid chicken! Again, she was correct. I did not prioritize others' feelings or their positions in the matter as I essentially threw my cook coworker under the bus by naming him while making amends. That was not my intent whatsoever, but that is what took place. My sponsor even suggested I was creating a "self-imposed crisis" out of all of this because from the beginning, she has only asked me to stay in prayer and remain willing—not to act. Especially, not to take impulsive action. Again, she was probably right as I resorted to crying over the heaviness of the weight I had given this amendment.

I consulted with another alcoholic. She reiterated my sponsor's words as well as stated that restitution still needed to be made in some form, whether it was staying on a shift longer or doing extra things for the restaurant like taking the trash out. Again, I prayed. I took no action.

My next shift, I felt anxiety in still wanting to make restitution, but I sat in my feelings and took no action. However, I did make amends to my coworker for making her uncomfortable and imposing my will. She told me I was overthinking the situation and asked if I wanted repayment of the money I spent on her food. I declined.

Days later, in an A.A. meeting, a member spoke about amendments and emphasized their significance. This member said, "A light from my Higher Power needs to shine on those issues." Making amends allows God's light to shine on the situation, on the feelings, and on the thoughts, and it clears everything away. Like a mushroom fungus that grows in the darkness of night but shrivels and dies in the light of day. Amendments are necessary to have God's light shine on the darkness and everything that grows in the darkness—fear, resentment, self-pity, helplessness. As I have stayed in prayer and have kept my eyes and ears open for God's will, I have decided that the right thing to do is pay full restitution. Even though the GM told me I did not need to, I think I do. My direct amends allowed some light to shine into the darkness, but some darkness remains still. I need to let His light fully shine. I need to make it completely right.

I shared the above sentiment with my sponsor, and she was all for it. I have learned from all of this that my tendency to want to complete something in its entirety and as quickly as I can, can hinder me and/ or the process of how something should be done. So I stayed patient and waited for the right opportunity to consult my GM about paying for the chicken. Because God has a sense of humor, the GM was out of town for the week. So wait, I did.

During the time the GM was out of town, there was food incorrectly made during my shift. A loaded baked potato. As soon as it became fair game amongst the staff, I was sure to get my hands on it. I boxed it up and placed it aside. I took a Step 10 personal inventory that I was in the right on obtaining this baked potato and not in my character defects. It was going to be thrown away, or someone else would have gotten it. It was not made just for me. My motives and intentions were honest. I would not need to deceive or manipulate anyone when I left with it in a to-go box.

At the end of my shift, I was going to buy some . . . yes . . . chicken to go on top of my baked potato. I waited for the bartender to return to the cash register to ring in my to-go order because she was somewhere else in the restaurant. One of the managers was standing close to me. After she asked me what I was going to order, she said, "Just chicken?" I laughed inside. I explained I had received an incorrectly made baked potato earlier in the shift and that I wanted to get some chicken to top it off and to add some protein.

She looked disgusted. I was confused because we sell loaded chicken baked potatoes all the time. I just wanted to recreate the dish we sell at the restaurant. She asked how long I had had the baked potato, and she explained that's why she was grossed out. She said I'm going to get sick one day eating food that is laid to the side, unrefrigerated, for hours.

Me and my part-time employed self responded, "Hey, it's free food."

She then asked me if I like my baked potato fully loaded and walked over to the kitchen area and told the cooks to make a fully loaded chicken baked potato. I was confused. Was I getting a free baked potato or was the manager just giving the back line a heads up about an upcoming order? The bartender still was not back so I walked to the manager and asked if this order was going to be rung in. "Not this time, Jessica."

So, grateful for a fresh loaded chicken baked potato, I asked her if she would feel better that I throw the one I had been saving in the trash. She said that she would, so in the trash it went.

What does this mean? God just gave me FREE CHICKEN. But I still needed to pay back for the other chicken I stole! Why would I be getting additional chicken that I am not paying for? Is this God's way of saying, "Chill, bro, we're good"? Did this mean I was out of the woods for my past chicken crime? Had I been forgiven?

I called my sponsor and explained I had not paid back the money yet for the stolen chicken and that I just received free chicken! She did not say I did not need to make it right any longer, but she did say that "right actions" and "having a willing attitude to do what's right" gets rewarded sometimes. *All right, fine. I will still pay for the chicken.*

Once the GM returned, and when I thought the appropriate moment arrived, I approached her. I asked her, "Do you remember the . . . the chicken confession?"

She laughed and asked if we could please call it "The Great Chicken Confession."

I loved the title and the overall vibe of the conversation. I told her in the confession I should have simply stuck to my side of the street and not named the cook that supplied the contraband—I mean, the chicken. Thankfully, she said she had not mentioned anything to the cook and implied she did not have intentions to. After thanking God for that, I told the GM, "Before, during The Great Chicken Confession, I asked you if I *had* to pay back the money for the chicken. Today, I am asking you if I *can* pay back the money for the chicken."

She replied, "You want to pay for the chicken?"

"Yes." My answer was mostly true. I wanted to make this right and let God's light fully shine in, but there was still a selfish side of me that wanted to move forward from this situation financially unscathed. But I was determined to make this right. She allowed me to pay for my mistakes, but she still gave me fifty percent off. I did not ask for my employee discount to be applied. I was prepared to pay for it in its entirety, but she automatically applied it. I paid for it in cash.

The freaking end.

~286 days sober to 311 days sober

MY JOURNEY TO RECOVERY

A NEW SONG

Sobriety

I have been in the program of Alcoholics Anonymous (A.A.) for twelve months and five days. I am 289 days sober (nine months and fourteen days). I ask myself, *How is sobriety working out for me?* That is a question I do not have to search for the answer to because it is so evident.

I am more spiritually fit. I have grown closer to my Higher Power, whom I call my God. I have learned how to give Him more of me and how to truly rely on Him.

I have grown in my emotional maturity. I have learned to accept both what the past has brought and what the present day brings. I have unpacked suitcases of emotional baggage and have sorted them out to their appropriate places. Alcoholics Anonymous has several promises that will come true in your life if you work the program as it is designed to the best of your ability. Promise number three states in the A.A. program, "We will not regret the past nor wish to shut the door on it."[58] In this process, I have released anger. I was aware of some anger I was carrying, but I was not aware of the suitcases of anger I was lugging around daily. With the help of God and this program, I have found and have felt peace like I have never felt before.

I am healthier and stronger. There are thirty-five pounds less of me to prove that! This is the most amount of weight I have ever lost in one period. I have never been so consistent in losing weight, nor have I ever lost weight over a one-year period. All my life I have fluctuated with my weight because in the past, I would get on a weight loss kick, and then I would get off for whatever reason. Then, back on and back off. I think this time has been different because I am not depriving myself, nor am I placing extra pressure on myself. I have simply made changes in my life to be healthier—healthier in my food and in my routine. Also, in this past year, I have realized that I used food and cutting as alternatives to alcohol. I used them to change how I was feeling. Since learning this, I have worked to change my relationship with food and with self-harm, in addition to my relationship with alcohol.

Glory be to God and the gifts He has given me. My relationships have more solidarity and more depth since getting sober. I am not

---

58. *Alcoholics Anonymous (4ᵗʰ ed.)—"The Big Book"* (2017), p. 83.

alone, nor have I ever been alone, despite what I have felt in the past. I am filled with gratitude and serenity. No, I do not always feel these positive emotions. Yes, situations happen, and convincing negative emotions are felt, but I stay in the darkness for shorter periods of time than before. Even times when I feel dead inside, I now have more tools to find my way out of the darkness. Even when I feel like I have no purpose in this life but to suffer, I have the knowledge to contradict these feelings. I have the knowledge and months of experience to understand that emotions and situations are temporary. My God is forever. I must rely on Him even when I feel like turning away. As my sponsor says, I must "suit up and show up" to meetings, to work, and to social events, even when I do not feel like it.

Another thing they say in the program is that my disease is doing push-ups and getting stronger while I am sober, waiting for me to relapse. I must continue to practice what I have learned, I must continue to attend meetings and participate in service work and fellowship with others, and I must stay close to my God in order to keep my disease of alcoholism at bay.

~290 days sober

The Last Tile

Throughout my childhood, I often assisted my dad in home improvement projects. One project was to replace the floor of the staircase landing from carpet to tile. My dad purchased the necessary supplies, including a few tiles to spare. One of my contributions to the project was to be the tile cutter. The tiles, in their entirety, did not fit perfectly into the allotted space. Thus, some tiles had to be cut. Just as in life and sobriety when I have had to adjust, develop, or leave behind unhealthy bits and pieces. I cut several pieces perfectly, and, again, just as in life, I cut some pieces jagged, leaving them unusable. But that was OK. I was learning, and there were tiles to spare.

Near the end, we were down to one tile, and it needed to be cut appropriately to fill the remaining space to complete the project. With the knowledge that I had cut other tiles unevenly, I second-guessed myself. I asked my dad if he would do it to ensure it would get done correctly. If done *incorrectly*, it would mean I failed and that the project would be delayed because we would have to go to the store for one additional tile. My dad refused. He had belief in my capabilities, whereas I did not. Leaning on his belief, I cut the tile . . . even! Perfect. I did it! What I accomplished in that moment was beyond the tile. It helped me believe in myself. My dad encouraged me to face my fear of failure instead of enabling my desire to avoid and, consequently, inflate my insecurities.

This story sticks out to me as I sit in an Alcoholics Anonymous meeting about belief in oneself and how that can turn into a negative. I could take my belief in myself and extend it to believing I have control over alcohol and over my life. To believe in myself is one thing. To believe I have control over my life and my drinking, that is an entirely separate thing. God is in control of my life. Controlling my alcohol intake is an ability I no longer possess, leaving me powerless and unable. As I practice self-confidence and as I improve my self-esteem, I must not become grandiose. I must keep in mind and keep in practice humility and surrendering to my Higher Power, to my God. A God that is beautiful and capable in every way. My God is helping me believe in myself the way my earthly father did years ago. God is showing me how to live a life of humility, serenity, and balance.

~292 days sober

Splat!

Skipping from one pink cloud to the next
Each one varying in shape and shade

Without realizing it
I misstep, and SPLAT!
Not only have I descended from the clouds
I did so in a painful way

The pink cloud is not an everlasting state
It is simply a state of elevation from time to time

Some falls from the pink clouds are gradual
Like descending in a hot air balloon from ten thousand feet to the ground
Other falls are like being pulled beneath from an undercurrent
Tumbling so quickly and violently I am not sure which direction I am headed

Regardless of the type of fall, the reason is typically the same
Humility
There are mistakes to be had
There are lessons to be learned

While I prefer my status up in the shades of pink
I must resume my life down below without a drink
If I give in to my disease
The pink clouds disappear
And storm clouds move in

Upon each fall
With every lesson learned
I must fall back on my tools that I have learned from the program
When I do this
I work my way back up to the clouds
After all, I feel closest to God up there

~295 days sober

And Now I Lay Me Down to Sleep . . .

In today's meeting, some of my fellow alcoholics are discussing how much their lives have improved since quitting the sauce. Some are sharing memories of active addiction—of waking up in another person's home, waking up to a strange car in the driveway, etcetera. I am reminded of times I would wake up in my own home and not know where I was. I might as well have woken up in someone else's home, based on how disoriented I was.

The times I woke up after blacking out and passing out, depending on how I felt, determined if I would drink more or not. Let me clarify. Even if my decision was to go to bed, I would still finish the drink that I was drinking before I passed out. Either way, going to bed or staying awake, I would still consume more. I do not remember choosing between whether I would finish the drink or not; it was just my reality, my lifestyle. It was what my disease had become.

Something sobriety has brought me is the knowledge of where I will wake up. Frankly, it has also brought me knowledge of where I will fall asleep. There is no question of if I will wake up in the kitchen, on the couch, in my bed, or on the floor of my home office. I did not get sober to remember where I will fall asleep or to know where I will awaken, but it certainly has been a positive consequence of sobriety.

~295 days sober

The Murky Depths

I am 295 days sober. Today, I reflect on the pool and the murky depths I immersed myself in almost 300 days ago. When I turn and look at the pool, I see things I had never noticed before. There is a "closed" sign on the fence. *Wait . . . there is a fence! I do not remember that before.* I also notice poison signs—skulls and crossbones—hung at various points around the fence. At the top of the fence, there is barbed wire. Thick, metal thorns meant to keep those inside and deter others from entering.

Cautiously, I walk closer to see the straws. Occasionally, I see someone come up for air from the murky depths of alcohol and alcoholism. I feel . . . I feel sadness. I feel despair for those trapped in the pool and trapped in our disease. Even if they wanted to leave, there are obstacles that discourage them from scaling the fence. The obstacles certainly deter me from re-entering.

I look to see if anyone is trying to get out. I have been told that if I want to keep my sobriety, I must give it away. I see no one trying to leave. I see no one looking for help. May God help them. May Thy will be done.[59] May God help me know who to help and when.

I turn back around. I focus on the twenty-four hours ahead of me, not the pain I suffered in the past. God, thank You for helping me out of the murky depths.

~295 days sober

Loss and Gains

I am still in disbelief that I have lost thirty-five pounds in one year. I know I have written a couple of times on this, but I am still processing this amazing byproduct of my sobriety. It is incredible that while weight loss was not my main focus, I have been able to lose more

---

59. *Alcoholics Anonymous (4th ed.)*—"*The Big Book*" (2017). Part of the Step 3 prayer on p. 63.

weight than any other time (which feels likes hundreds of times) in my life. I have learned, during my time in A.A., new depths of unhealthy choices I was making and their ugly consequences. I have learned to make healthier, smarter decisions, and amazing consequences have been the result. As mentioned, thirty-five pounds less of me. An amazing 295 days of sobriety. A rejuvenated relationship with God. A new network of friends. Renewed relationships with family. A rehabilitated relationship with myself.

~296 days sober

Freedom From . . . Freedom To
Daily Reflection: January 30

The reflection states, "I will begin to know a 'new' freedom; not the old freedom of doing what I pleased, without regard to others, but the new freedom that allows fulfillment of the promises in my life. What a joy it is to be free!"[60]

The reading is true. I had come to regard *freedom* as the ability to choose for myself and do whatever the heck I wanted to do. I felt a freedom when I left a past job. I felt free when I got a divorce (but shortly after, I was trapped again by my blossoming alcoholism). I still feel a freedom when I have honored a commitment and the event/situation is complete. That is because I am a homebody and I continue to struggle with socializing in any regard outside the rooms of A.A. and outside the confines of work. I felt freedom when I could drink as much as I wanted and drink it however fast I wanted. I was free when I was alone with my drink.

I have heard for the past year in these meetings that I will know a new freedom. But today it rings in a different meaning. In choosing sobriety today, I choose freedom. Freedom from bondage to the bottle. Freedom from planning everything around the drink. I have the freedom to be myself. My honest, genuine self. This sober person I have come to know and love. I have the freedom to be a sober dog mom. A sober employee. A sober child of God. A free, humble servant in my faith.

Before I got sober, I was a dog mom. I was an employee. I was some of the things I mentioned. But today, *today*, I am free to enjoy these

---

60. *Daily Reflections* (2016), p. 38.

roles more. I am free to give more of myself to these roles. I have the freedom to thank God for what I have. I have the freedom to ask God that His will be done. It is hard to explain in words what is felt in essence. It is something in my soul that is different. It is the new freedom "The Big Book" describes and promises.[61] I am grateful today for this freedom.

~301 days sober

Job Hunt

I have been looking for a full-time job for three months now, and the only bite I have gotten was from a pyramid-scheme-like marketing firm. I am a licensed professional counselor, so that is not exactly in my field! It has been discouraging. But I have persisted with applying for jobs. I began looking outside of driving distance and have applied for jobs in Hilton Head, SC, and Savannah, GA.

I misunderstood an application, and I applied for a job in Metter, GA. Do not even ask me where that is. I have lived in Georgia for eighteen years and have never heard of Metter, GA! It was also for a position I needed to learn more about to know if I would even want it. Well, they liked me enough to want an interview. It gave me forty-eight hours to pray and think about pros and cons of relocating, just in case they like me.

The next day, I got a call from a recruiter for an in-person interview for a treatment center in Gainesville, GA! A city I used to work in and one that was within driving distance. And it was for an intake position that I really wanted. I went from zero interviews to two in two days! What a blessing.

One job seems scary because I would have to relocate. One job seems perfect because it is in a location I like for a position I want. A difference in me, I am noticing, is that I am not telling God which job I want. Frankly because I do not have either job yet, and I don't want to get ahead of myself. Also, I am asking God that His will be done. His plans are always better than mine. I also pray to express gratitude for these opportunities.

~302 days sober

---

61. *Alcoholics Anonymous (4ᵗʰ ed.)—"The Big Book"* (2017), p. 83.

In My Skin

I am so grateful for where I am today. "The Big Book" story called, "My Chance to Live," was read in the meeting this morning. The story states, "Today, I fit in my skin" (*Alcoholics Anonymous*, p. 318). A little over a year ago, I hated my own skin. So much so that I was on the verge of killing my skin and the pathetic soul it encapsulated.

Today, I have an interview for which I am beyond excited and grateful. I feel comfortable in my own skin. More than ever before, I feel my outsides match my insides. The weight loss has helped me feel more comfortable physically, sure. But psychologically, I am in a completely different headspace. For as much as I need income, and for as much as I think I would love this job, I am not begging God to get me this job today. Instead, I am asking that His will be done. I am more than qualified for the position I am interviewing for today. Also, I tend to do well in interviews. I am confident in my capabilities. Thus, the outcome is truly in God's hands. I know that if I do not get this job, it simply is not meant to be. This is not to say it ever wasn't in His hands. I am meaning that I have applied for some jobs the last few months that I questioned if I was qualified for. With this job today, I know I am qualified. So if it doesn't work out, I know it is simply not meant to be. I feel, with where I am in my spiritual life, I can accept that without throwing a pity party. Only time will tell!

~306 days sober

29th Birthday

I am officially twenty-nine years old today. The Daily Reflection for my birthday states, "I should seek to do His will by living spiritual principles and my reward will be sanity and emotional sobriety."[62] If I could ask for a birthday gift, it would be sanity and emotional sobriety! Even before I knew it, I was searching for emotional sobriety. And I have been chasing sanity for over a decade. Today, it is a gift to realize that I am the sanest I have ever been, and I am the closest to emotional sobriety that I have ever been.

---

62. *Daily Reflections* (2016), p. 45.

So far this morning, I have been celebrating my birthday in a way a lot of people would consider boring, but that does not matter. I recorded the State of the Union Address last night. This morning, I have been watching the speech while working on my puzzle. I ate a healthy breakfast. I did my morning prayers and reflection. I feel whole. I feel filled. I feel content. I enjoy keeping up with the news. I love working on my puzzles. I love how my dogs sit near me when I work on puzzles. I do not need alcohol today to celebrate my birthday.

It is an interesting day in general, to receive congratulations and praise for simply being born—something entirely out of my control. But today, being 10 months and 1 day sober (307 days), I am choosing to celebrate "my day" by doing activities that I enjoy without causing harm to myself. My brother and sister-in-law have invited me over for dinner tonight. I can speak confidently that I will be sober for dinner. I can speak with definitiveness that I will be able to drive to their house for dinner. I can speak with certainty that my family will support me and won't drink in my presence. I can speak with self-assuredness that I will be able to drive home safely *not* under the influence and *not* taking back roads thinking it would lessen my chances of getting pulled over.

Thank You, God, for introducing me to Alcoholics Anonymous thirteen months ago. The progress I have made with You, with my sanity, with my life, with my family, with my perceptions, with my social network, with myself—thank You from the bottom of my twenty-nine-year-old heart. I love You.

~307 days sober

My Frosty

My sweet baby girl . . . my fourteen-year-old miniature schnauzer/ chihuahua cranky old lady . . . my ride or die . . . my Frosty Girl . . . my partner in crime since I was fifteen years old.

Just as it is said by old-timers to newcomers in sobriety, "This too shall pass," and "time heals all wounds." But what about the wounds that time creates? Frosty was once a pup. She was full of life, with a sassy, alpha attitude. Granted, she still has her moments, but her old-lady-ness has kicked into high gear over the past year. Once starving for breakfast, she now chooses her heating pad over her morning meal. Once getting up with me when the alarm goes off, now she does not hear the alarm or me when I get out of bed. Once able to follow me around, regardless of the circumstance, now she requires light to move because cataracts make it impossible to see in the dark. Once jumping onto structures with ease, now she has three sets of doggy stairs spread throughout the house.

In the fourteen years I have had this dog, I have graduated high school, I have gotten both my bachelor's and master's degrees, I have gotten married and divorced, and I have moved all around. Besides God and my family's love, my little Frosty has been my constant. She has been the ultimate companion. Frankly, she makes the rules in the house, and I and the other two dogs live by them!

I was told at the vet yesterday that she has dementia. My heart broke. I did not know a dog could get such a condition, but the evidence is right before my eyes. Frosty will leave me on the couch, go to the kitchen to get water, and then forget where I am. She will travel upstairs and go in and out of the three bedrooms searching for me. She will do this and other things that pain my heart as her mother.

She also has issues with her spine. Three bones of her spine are fusing together as one bone, causing her significant pain. So much pain the doc is recommending a treatment he cannot legally sell me in my state yet: hemp CBD essential oil. Not from a cannabis plant but from a hemp plant.

I could drink over this. Thirteen months ago I would have drunk over this. Such a good excuse! *My dog is dying.* If she's not necessarily dying, her quality of life is going downhill. I won't keep her alive just to suffer. I pray this oil can help. Instead of reaching for the bottle, I am reaching to God. I am being present with my Frosty. I am being available. I am being a responsible dog mom. I would hate to drink and then not remember any of my last moments with her.

Thus, time can both create and heal wounds. It is double-sided, I suppose. Time heals the wounds it creates. I am grateful for the time I have left with her. I have been blessed with this amazing canine whom I have had the pleasure of sharing half of my life with.

~307 days sober

Hi, My Name is Jessica, and I am a Foodaholic

Sometimes, while I am in the middle of something, it is hard to recognize how bad it truly is. I have not been OK. I have fallen back into the trap of using a substance to change the way I feel—food. I think it started off as menstrual, and then it morphed into stress eating for the two interviews that I had within a week's time. Then, of course, I had to celebrate how well I did on the interviews . . . so pizza and wings it was!

In hindsight, those used to be some of my favorite drinking foods. On this day specifically, I overate, and I felt sick. The next morning, I felt hungover from getting drunk off of the food. I was decent on food consumption the next day, just like I used to maybe go lighter on drinking the day after a big binge. I have been on this cycle for two weeks. Feeling desperate, I turned to God to relieve me from this bondage to food.

Today, I woke up at 4 a.m., and I had to make a decision: go back to sleep and stay on this unhealthy track, or get my butt up and be healthy. By the grace of God, I chose the latter. I took my dogs for a walk around the neighborhood. I have selfishly been denying my dogs a walk for a week . . . something I also did when I was drinking. Afterwards, I went to the gym, then a meeting. One step at a time, I will get back on my healthy track.

"The Big Book" explains the phenomenon of craving with drinking. After one drink, you crave more and more and cannot stop. That is what has happened with me these past couple of weeks with food. Food was not my only thought. Of course, I thought about drinking again. In the past, I used to prepare for interviews by drinking red wine the night before and rehearsing answers to pretend interview questions. Both then and now, I also wanted to celebrate after my interviews. I had a birthday. I was faced with my dog's mortality and inevitable death. I have dealt with these things well in the moment, but I also think they have been adding up. So, yeah, alcohol has been a reoccurring thought, but it has not been a craving. I walked away from the murky depths a while ago, but I still find myself driving around the fence sometimes, thinking about re-entering. I thought about all the alcohol substitutes I have used before. I thought about binging on energy drinks. I thought about cutting. I resisted them all except for food. I rationalized it as being a more acceptable way to change the way I feel.

Honestly, during these past couple of weeks, I have felt great. Other times, I have tried to fit my butterfly body back into its cocoon, hoping to go backwards and be a caterpillar again. Sometimes success and good times are just as stressful and scary as bad times. But a butterfly, I am. I cannot and will not go back.

As I reflect on the past two weeks, I see how consumed I was with wanting to change how I felt. For as much money as I do not have, I even spent money on Amazon one day, hoping the dopamine would calm the anxiety I was feeling. This morning, I am grateful to have given the dogs what they deserve. I did my Daily Reflection, which pointed out, "Regular attendance at meetings, serving and helping others is the recipe that many have tried and found to be successful. Whenever I stray from these basic principles, my old habits resurface, and my old self also comes back with all its fears and defects."[63] That explains why I have been going back to my old habits of wanting to change how I feel. With things going on lately, I have been inconsistent with my meeting attendance. I have been inconsistent with my service to others. And my sleep has been inconsistent. I am going to contact my psychiatrist about that. If I look back on my fourteen-year history with insomnia, I can identify countless times where my sleep getting off track created a domino effect of many things getting off track.

I am grateful that I can identify and analyze this now, two weeks in, before gaining more momentum on the unhealthy track that I was on that would eventually lead back to the drink.

~310 days sober

Shakespeare

My morning motivation today is a Shakespearean quote, stating, "The fool doth think he is wise, but the wise man knows himself to be a fool."[64] I have most definitely gained wisdom over the past year because I have come to know myself to be an addicted fool. I believed I could control my drinking. My blackouts and embarrassing

---

63. *Daily Reflections* (2016), p. 47.
64. William Shakespeare, *As You Like It.*

moments taught me that this was not the case. I have learned that this fool is incredibly loved by my secular family and friends and my amazing Father above.

I used to think I was wise. But that wisdom led me to the pool and its alcoholic, murky depths. Now, in admitting I am a fool, I am wiser than ever before. In admitting I am not in control, the more I feel in control. Because when I let God be in control, I am not burdened with stress regarding the outcome. In the humblest of ways, I suppose I have become a "wise (wo)man" because I am *well* aware of how much of a fool I can be!

~312 days sober

Drunken Mistakes

Due to my isolative tendencies, I have mostly avoided drunken mistakes with others. This is not to say there aren't things I would and should have done differently if I had been sober. However, compared to some things I have heard from other alkies, I would say my tendency to isolate and self-destruct kept me away from destroying relationships with those around me. I have learned in my sobriety that my reclusive tendencies were hurtful in themselves, and I have since made amends to others for that . . . but this is not the point I am trying to make right now.

A dear friend of mine that is not an alcoholic told me of something she did while heavily under the influence. Something she would never have done sober or even tipsy when she still has some wits about her. She only has flashes of what happened and has had an emotional hangover that has far exceeded her physical one.

It makes me stop and reflect. I think back to how my other friend was scared I had killed myself because I did not answer my door (because I was blacked-out, passed-out drunk). I think of the "yets," as they say in the program—of the destruction that a person has *yet* to encounter but surely will if s/he continues his/her life in active alcoholism. These *yets* are institutions, incarceration, or death. This can be death of oneself or the death of someone else (e.g., driving drunk).

I wonder what *yets* I am avoiding by staying sober. At this time, I am not curious enough to find out.

~314 days sober

Taste of the Past: Part I

A couple of times lately, I have had the taste of a vodka cranberry drink in my mouth. It just pops up out of nowhere, and dang it tastes good. The taste brings with it memories of happiness, carelessness, enjoyment, and a specific type of freedom. I foolishly entertain these thoughts, and then I think, *What is this? Am I back to day 11? White knuckled as I pray to God to relieve me from the phenomenon of craving? Am I doing something wrong? Have I done something wrong?*

No, I have not done a thing wrong. A thought is only a thought. An action, however, is something entirely different. If I chose (action) to continue entertaining those thoughts and then go to the store to pick up vodka and juice (action), I would not be 313 days sober to write this today. As quick as the taste of the past comes to my mouth, I am able to move forward and leave the past in the past.

~313 days sober

Zero Alcohol Contents

Seriously? Heineken? Heineken 0.0 now exists. The brew allegedly goes through an alcohol removal process and contains zero alcohol. I was never a big beer drinker, but I will not lie—when I saw the commercial advertising Heineken 0.0, I immediately thought I needed that in my life. Indulge my logic: I could drink the stuff, and I would test out the theory of the placebo effect. I could convince myself that it *does* contain alcohol and have a good time doing whatever the frack I wanted! Like the good ole days! But it does not actually contain any alcohol, so I would not have to start over in my sobriety! I would not have to pick up a white chip! Genius!

Silly alcoholic brain. Could I truly test out the placebo effect if I am aware of the placebo? After I allowed my logic to justify drinking beer again, I got real with myself. That stuff would just be a gateway to actual alcohol. I would go from 0.0 percent to 80 proof in no time flat!

~315 days sober

Consequences

Well, crap. The thirty-five-pound weight loss was nice, but due to my choices as of late, I have put back on nearly four pounds. *Uugghh.* Gaining weight back is one of my worst fears. It is time to get back on track. It is time to stop using food and energy drinks to change the way I feel. It is time to practice extra self-care. I cannot guarantee that my alcoholic brain won't take this on as a personal problem to become obsessed with . . . but we will see.

~318 days sober

Offer Accepted

It has officially happened. God has continued to provide for me. I got a job! A job where I can finally afford my life! Time to celebrate, right? But, how? Hmm. Of course, my initial thought is getting a pre-chilled, big-ole bottle of Moscato—regular, pink, or red, it does *not* matter. That would just be the warmup while my vodka is chilling in the freezer. Probably grapefruit or pomegranate flavor and some diet cranberry or diet pomegranate juice (I may be a foodaholic, but I still like to cut calories where I can).

Obviously, my thoughts were getting a little too carried away with that. So I called some fellow alkies to tell them the good news and how I wished to celebrate. One alky and I commiserated over the isolation we used to do while drinking—how we would create our own happy place and shut out the rest of the world and do whatever the heck we wanted. There would be nothing to get in the way and no one around to judge. We said one of the greatest parts of drinking was the *escapism.* But why, in this instance, would I want to escape? I want to share! I just don't know how to celebrate sober. Another alcoholic compadre said, "We celebrate by sharing our joy with others." Little did I realize I was celebrating already, and I did not even know it! This particular alky was the fifth person I called.

I thought of celebrating by getting a celebratory meal. Heck no! I am still digging myself out of the almost four-pound hole I dug myself into when I "celebrated" a couple of weeks ago.

Hold up! I did not even mention the most important way I celebrated. I first celebrated by thanking God and by expressing how grateful I am for this opportunity. But my addicted brain wants more. More of anything to elate me—alcohol, food, energy drinks, something!

After my phone calls, I asked God to release me from bondage of self. I celebrated in a way I never have in my adult life. I took care of myself by going to a meeting, working out, showering, praying, reaching out to others, and eating healthy all day. I took care of my four-legged children by taking them on a walk, taking my old lady Frosty to get her nails trimmed, and buying them some tasty treats to enjoy.

God's will is something else. It truly is powerful. I feel confident that this job is meant for me because I have been praying for His will to be done for months. It feels like His will for me was to get this job. It feels like it's His will that I was given another chance to celebrate something good, and I took care of myself instead of destroying myself. Progress!

~321 days sober

Capsized: Part II

Before, on day 41 when I capsized, I did not know where anyone or anything else was. I was only concerned about my own self drowning in the liquid that was ultimately killing me. *Where was my family? Where were my dogs? Did everything in my life fall out of that boat?* I cannot tell you where everything went as I floated in that ocean of alcohol, but I can tell you that everything has since reappeared.

After floating in the life jacket for what seemed like ages, a new boat appeared. Not new as in a brand-new boat but new as in it was new to me, and it was floating upright. My sponsor was on board. My family, my friends, and my dogs were all on board, but they remained in the far end of the boat. My sponsor helped me out of the ocean.

Aboard, I shriveled into the fetal position and over-contemplated everything. *Did I really just resist the liquid god I had come to know and love? Am I really giving it up? Why are my family, friends, and dogs so far away? Can they see me like this? I want to be close to them. I want to be far from them. I want to stay aboard this boat forever. I want to jump back into the ocean and drink until I black out. I want to stay in and live. I want to jump out and die.* The thoughts went on and on.

The longer I lied there, the more coherent I became. My dogs sensed this and ventured across the boat to visit me. Frosty led the pack, Frankie and Buster followed behind. *How could they still love someone as disgusting and as pathetic as me?* I didn't care. I embraced their love. My friends and family remained afar.

My sponsor encouraged me to come to the middle of the boat where other people had appeared. I was handed books called *Alcoholics Anonymous* ("The Big Book") and the *Twelve Steps and Twelve Traditions* ("The 12 & 12"). People shared, and I listened. When I had the courage to share, they listened. I read. My sponsor and I talked. In between these meetings I would send messages to my family. I would write to them and let them know how I was doing. I still could not see past myself at this point. They would write back and then continue on with whatever they were doing at the other end of the boat.

The day came when I had the courage to approach them. To tell them I loved them. To apologize for my absence and any other trespasses. They embraced me. My brother asked me to start showing up to things instead of calling out. I promised to try. Months later, he wrote me: "Thank you very much for your help lately. I really appreciate how you have been so available to help." From being an absent member swimming in the ocean, floating in the ocean, staying far away at the end or the middle of the boat, to being acknowledged for my continued presence in the family as a sister, a daughter, and an auntie . . . wow.

~323 days sober

The Time Has Come

How can multiple emotions be felt all at once? And how can they be felt so purely, so fully all at once? This morning, I am taking Frosty to put her in everlasting sleep. I have an overwhelming conviction that her time has come. When her Frosty feistiness has gone from frequent to rare form . . . when I cannot touch her lower half without her moving away in pain . . . I believe her time has come. I have been beside myself with emotions. Again, how can I feel such a variety of emotions so purely? I feel deep and heavy despair. I feel heartwarming joy as I have my final moments with her. I feel the pain of worries of "what ifs." I am overwhelmed with gratitude for this life we have been able to share together. I feel respect for the fourteen-year-old cranky lady that she is. I feel honored she chose me to be her person . . . her number one (besides herself—she did love herself an awful lot).

I feel pride for the big sister she was to Buster. I am concerned about how he will move forward without her. As for Frankenstein (Frank or Frankie, for short), Frosty has more of an unwanted stepsister relationship with her. Frosty has always felt threatened by Frankie's alpha nature. Instead of showing her vulnerable side, Frosty chooses to show her butt instead and picks silly fights with Frank. But, oh, how Frankie loves Frosty and just wants to be best friends with her. One time, another dog picked a fight with Frankie and had Frankie pinned to the ground. You better believe Frosty was leading her and Buster's counterassault on the dog to let Frankie up. It was in that moment that her true love for Frankie was shown. Frosty has her own signature way of showing love to certain people. For the longest time before she became old, Frosty and my brother got along by riding on his six-foot-six-inch shoulders. She enjoyed the view and altitude up there.

I have had the honor of having this dog since freshman year of high school. She helped me get through high school, through college, through marriage and divorce, through starting my career, and through getting sober. Now, as I am about to start a new chapter of my life with a new job, I think I need her more than ever. I need our next chapter to continue the story between me and one of the greatest loves of my life. But that is not how it is going to be. I can imagine her telling me that I am strong enough now to go into the next chapter without her. That it is her time to be with God. That it is her time to be in heaven and to be the alpha to all the dogs already there.

All right, Frosty girl. Go be with God. Say, "Hi," to Casi, Roxy, and Bama for me. Don't forget, Bama gets really annoyed at your little chihuahua bark. Keep that in mind as you go to rule the dogs in heaven. I love you.

~Mommy, 324 days sober

I Will See You Again

This morning, I held you
My hand cupped your chest

Boom boom
I felt your heart beat

Hours later
Still holding you
Your heart went silent
I held you close to my chest
Hoping yours would hear mine and your heart would remember
how to beat
It didn't

Away you went
To a happier place
You're no longer in pain
You get to see Roxy, Casi, and Bama again

Buster, Frankie, and I are all sad
You were our leader, after all
But we will be OK
Knowing you're no longer in pain you never deserved
Your body held on for fourteen years
But it was time to let it all go

Live on, my Frosty girl
I will see you again
Where we will become inseparable,
Like we were since day one

~Mommy, 324 days sober

The Hole in My Heart

In days since Frosty's passing, when I have been around other people, I have often wondered, *Can they tell there is a hole in my heart?* My other thought, as days have passed, is that this is the healthiest I have ever coped, ever, with anything. I was selfless in relieving Frosty from the pain she was in. And, as difficult as it was, I held her as her soul left earth and ascended towards heaven. I always anticipated, when this day came, that my life would abruptly stop. I thought the earth would stop spinning. I thought my lungs would quit breathing. I never would have imagined that I was capable enough to cope with this. As I am continuing to grieve, I am continuing to live life. No one is more surprised than me. In early, early sobriety, I remember thinking, *If Frosty dies then I will drink again.*

I have continued to work. I have continued to communicate with others. I even went out with friends due to a commitment I made before her passing. I have continued . . . period. Sometimes, I still lay down and play a memory reel in my mind of Frosty's greatest moments. Sometimes I cry. Other times I smile. Sometimes I do both.

Stories have come to mind that I have heard from meetings and from talking with other alcoholics this past year. Months ago, there was someone in my home group who lost their long-time love doggie. He was so upset, but he gave an inspirational speech about how he wasn't going to drink over his grief. He shared how he was choosing to feel his feelings, as difficult as they were. I also thought of an alcoholic friend who shared her story with me. She shared that in the first year of her sobriety, she lost her son. Someone she knew way longer than fourteen years. Still, she did not drink. If these people lost important people and pets in their lives and still didn't drink, how could I use this as a reason (excuse) to drink?

With a couple of hours left of Frosty's life, I promised her I would not let her death destroy me. I have every intention of keeping that promise. Drink, I have not! Fourteen months ago, I would have handled this *so* differently. Back then, I would have only leant on myself, the bottle, and my therapist. Now, I am leaning on God, my friends, my family, and my two other fur babies. As a mental health therapist and as a therapy attendee, I am all for counseling! But I have not needed to call and move up my next appointment because I have been OK. I have been hurting, I have been sad, but I, with God's help, have been able to manage. I have been to meetings three out of the past five days. I accepted a dinner invitation I did not feel like going to but am glad I did. I am meeting with my sponsor today. I am not alone. I am letting go and letting God run the show. What a relief that I am not in charge of everything. I can grieve and live simultaneously. Something I was never capable of before I got sober.

~329 days sober

Deception

The deception of the sauce is mighty and strong
What I thought was an angel was really a devil
What I thought breathed life into me sucked it out of me
What I thought gave me a purpose to live was, in truth, giving
me a reason to die

What I thought vs. what I now know
I know to drink is to die
I know it can only deceive me if I allow it
I know if I keep my reliance on God . . .
If I keep taking right action . . .
If I keep lowering my expectations . . .
If I keep attending meetings . . .
If I maintain fellowship . . .
If I do service work . . .

I will not be deceived

~330 days sober

Taste of the Past: Part II

It's happened again
The taste for the sauce
For the booze, the hooch, the hard stuff
Whatever you want to call it
I tasted it

I was thinking of how I am to return to a full-time job soon
And, when I was working full-time before,
I enjoyed coming home and cooking while sipping on a glass of red wine
Then sipping on a glass through dinner
Then sipping on a glass after dinner
. . . until bedtime . . .
During which time I felt like a modern-day single working woman
I could work, make my own food, and hold my liquor (and wine)

There I go again with my alcoholic brain
I am thinking of the "good" or putting a good spin on the past,
    romanticizing my drinking
I don't think of how the red wine part became the most important
    part of my nighttime routine . . .
. . . which led to hangovers
No one, even an alcoholic, cares to have a hangover
Then vodka and cranberry juice became my regular
My nighttime routine as a "modern-day working woman" slowly
    became uglier and uglier

Ugh.
Time to do things differently.
I'll just flavor my water, if anything.
Feeling healthier feels too good to give it up for a drink.

~332 days sober

11 Months

Eleven. E-l-e-v-e-n. 11. 1-1. Wow! Eleven months! It is such a blessing. It is so powerful how I have had major life changes lately, how I have experienced some "tastes of the past," and yet I have remained sober through it all!

My latest trigger has not even led me back to the bottle, although I have certainly thought about it: my new job.

I was bumped to the orientation after next because I am on a "medical hold." My drug test results have not come back yet, so the hospital was forced to delay my start date by two weeks. They outsource their drug tests, so my urine is somewhere in someone's lab just waiting to be tested! It is ironic, in a way. A sober alky is getting her start date delayed because of a drug test. My sponsor reminded me that we do not know God's plans or reasons but that there is one. That was true, of course. Still, I was disappointed.

That disappointment quickly turned into concern about money. I have been accruing debt because my income has not been enough to support my living expenses. That same day, hours later, I got my tax refund check in the mail for $2,300! The Lord provides! If I budget well and if I do not have extra expenses, that can cover my cost of living for a whole month!

Time to sit back, enjoy my eleven-month anniversary, and know that God has my back. I will try to pick up shifts at the restaurant the next two weeks to make some more money and to keep busy. Getting a job is triggering in itself because I want to drink to celebrate! So I need to stay focused and keep busy and keep working my program!

~335 days sober

From Student to Attendee

In my meeting today, my share reflected on my first experiences with Alcoholics Anonymous. Thanks to an assignment from my substance abuse course in grad school, I attended two A.A. meetings as a student learning about alcoholism and alcoholism treatment. Four years later, I entered the rooms as someone who desperately needed help.

When I attended my first meeting as an alcoholic, I was so warmly welcomed. I was applauded and praised for picking up a white chip. I did not understand it at the time. I was embraced and surrounded by women after the meeting, giving me both their phone numbers and their encouragement. Someone invited me to a meeting the next day, and, just like that, I became a regular attendee. I am so grateful for *all* my experiences with A.A.

~338 days sober

Spaceship

Whenever I was down or suicidal in the past couple of years, I would listen to Kesha's song, "Spaceship." I related to the lyrics of not fitting in and just wanting to leave earth. Maybe not die, but just take my dogs and go somewhere else where I could not hurt myself or anyone else. Or, somewhere I could hurt myself where I would be removed enough from others and maybe not hurt them. Either way, I was suffering. I just wanted me and my dogs to go away. To go somewhere with no responsibility, no accountability, no relationships . . . sweet nothing. I was suffering from the powerlessness over my addiction. It was eating away at me and had reached my core. As my soul was being eaten alive (rather, drowned alive?), I wanted a spaceship to come and get me.

I imagine if I had gotten onto a spaceship and somehow attended meetings and gotten sober. I would be radioing down to earth right now: "Houston? You there? Houston? I need help. I am floating alone. I don't want to be alone anymore. I am done with self-pity, isolating, and relentless suffering. Can anyone hear me? Over."

I see the world much differently now that I am sober. I want to go back to earth. I want to be around my family and friends. I want to live. I want to be alive.

~341 days sober

Gratitude

Today is my ex-husband's birthday. I had forgotten until my phone so kindly reminded me. Two years ago, I bought a birthday cake and celebrated his birthday as a self-imposed therapeutic activity. I wanted to frame the day as a positive one, and despite how angry and hurt I was, I wanted to send positive vibes his way. Of course, I drank. What celebration is complete without alcohol? My past self would have said that, anyway.

This morning, when my phone reminded me of his birthday, I stopped what I was doing and prayed for him and his family. I prayed that he has happiness and peace in his day and that God's will would be done. Oh, the progress I have made in two years' time!

The topic of my meeting today was gratitude. I had plenty to share. I shared how I have been so surprised but so grateful for the perspective I have had on Frosty's death. I have been able to focus on the amazing life I had with that little girl. I can see how blessed I was to have her at all, let alone for fourteen years of my life.

I also shared about my niece and nephew, my Smalls and my Bearimus. Yesterday, my parents were planning to go out of town once my brother picked up his kids (the grandkids). Prior to yesterday, my mom and I had discussed me coming over once I left the restaurant, but she had decided, due to timing, it would be pointless for me to do so.

Yesterday, I was tired and hungry, and I was relieved to be cut from my shift because I could go home, eat dinner, and lounge. I got to my car, relieved my plans for the day were basically done, and then I get a text from my mom: *What time do you think you'll be cut?* My reaction: *No no no no no no no no! Do I tell her I am already cut? Do I lie and say, "I don't know"? Ugh! Of course, I cannot lie. But I just want to go home and relax!* I called my sponsor and she didn't answer. I was not in a good head space! My character defects were being *directly* challenged. In that moment, I just wanted to focus on my mom's character defects . . . because *that* would certainly help the situation! Pshh. I prayed and was quiet. I thought of how I ask God each morning to make known to me His plan for me that day and for the willingness and the strength to follow through with it. With *His plan,* not mine. So willing, I was. Partially resentful, but willing, I told my mom I had been cut from the restaurant. She asked me to come and watch the grandkids until my brother was available to pick them up. It's not that it was a big deal to go and help, it was just that my mind and heart were already set on my plans for the afternoon. One of my character defects is inflexibility. Once I have a plan set, I really struggle with last minute changes. Realllllly struggle. But, I am willing!

I showed up to her house, and the resentment was written all over my face. But I was there to be of service regardless. I am willing!

My resentment quickly faded as my little Bearimus and Smalls acknowledged me: "Hey! J's here!"

I was going to watch them for one and a half hours, but then that turned into three hours. I am present enough in these kids' lives now that they are comfortable with me. It used to be that Auntie J was the golden family relative and the kids would do whatever I asked. Now that I am around more often, I hold less of a golden stature and am more of a commoner amongst the other family members. A consequence of this is that the kids are now comfortable enough to show their butts to me and do not always listen.

The reason I bring this whole thing up is that despite the negative attitude I had at first, and despite my niece and nephew becoming rebellious around me more frequently, I love them so much. I had moments of gratitude sprinkled in throughout the evening. And I feel tons of gratitude in hindsight. Little Bearimus has become quite the climber, and he, as little kids do, fell off something. He first cried for "Daddy" but then realized I was the only option, so he clung to me and cried out his feelings. Once the crying ended, he laid in my lap and rested against my legs. I took a picture of it to capture the greatness of the moment. I have been present enough in this little man's life that he trusts me to comfort him when he is sad or hurt, and he trusts me enough to be vulnerable and lay his head to rest in my embrace. That is a moment I never would have had if I had been at home lounging in my self-will. Because I was willing, I had this moment. My Higher Power, this program, my sponsor, my family, and my friends, have made everything I have written about today possible. It is a beautiful thing.

~343 days sober

God's Plan

I ask each morning that God show His plans for me today and that He give me the willingness and the strength to follow through with them. I ask for the strength to follow His will, not mine.

I have been anxiously and excitedly waiting to start my new job. My start date was already delayed two weeks due to some complications with the drug test, so my new start date was coming up. Things are on track as I got the notification a day or two ago that I was finally cleared to start! Yesterday, I got an email from my new boss basically saying, *Hey, by the way, there is an orientation tomorrow from 8–12:30. I'm not sure if you were told about that.*

No! I wasn't. I was more than fine with that though. I asked if I was able to attend even though I had not gone to the general and clinical orientation at the hospital yet. She said I could. I was excited that I would get to start a few days early! I cancelled my plans for the next day. I had a therapy appointment and a shift at the restaurant. Cancel, I did! Excitement!

It is the morning of orientation, and I am excited and ready. I tried on different clothes to wear for my first day, something that is normally a chore to go through, but I am excited because I am able to put a lot of clothes in a "too big" stack to go into the attic later. I take a picture of my dressed-up self and sent a text to my family, stating, *Grateful to be sober and to have this wonderful opportunity of a job! First day of orientation! Super excited! I love you all. Thank you for all of your support helping me build myself back up and getting to this moment!* I was ready.

My new place of employment is just down the road from my previous place of full-time employment. Therefore, the drive to Gainesville,

GA, at 7:30 a.m. was not new. On my way to work, I had some crazy, insane urges to drink. I even had some alcoholic thinking of, *Orientation only lasts until 12:30. I could drink the rest of the day and would not have to work again until Monday!* What the crap? I am almost a year sober! Excitement and some anxiety were mixed in with that strangeness. I tried praying, distracting, and refocusing myself. It was working.

I passed my old place of employment. I passed the liquor store across the street from where I worked. It was an old gas station that had gone out of business and a liquor store moved in. It was awfully convenient back when I was drinking. It took me back to memories of several years before. I remembered how I initially resisted going to the liquor store because, (1) I worked across the street as mental health therapist for children and adolescents, and (2) I had a very distinct-looking car at that time and could be easily recognized by passing cars and clients. As the story goes with addiction, my resistance did not last long. It was just too convenient. I remember leaving the office some days during lunch to go and buy vodka. I would walk in and out as quickly as possible, convinced it minimized the risk of someone seeing me. I then kept the bottle underneath my driver's seat, so if anyone looked in my car in the parking lot at work, it would not be seen. Of course I considered it, but I quit this job before I got to the point of drinking during the work day. I simply would feel more at ease knowing that I had an alcohol supply for the evening.

Thus, when I passed this place *today,* I had the harrowing memories of jeopardizing my job while going to buy alcohol while still on the clock. And I also had an incredible realization. In the back of my car were two car seats from babysitting my niece and nephew yesterday. In two years' time, I have gone from hiding alcohol underneath my seat to being present and trusted to be around and babysit my niece and nephew. I felt gratitude and thanked God for my progress.

After that unwelcomed stroll down memory lane, I got to orientation. Then, I was turned away. The ladies in the front office told me I was not allowed to attend that specific orientation until I completed the general and clinical orientation at the hospital. I told them that my boss was aware of my orientation status and still cleared me to attend this orientation today. They tried contacting my boss but were unable to. They told me it was the rules of the hospital. This was not rejection, just a miscommunication. Still, it felt like rejection. Dealing with rejection sober is not my strongest suit.

I get back to my car, and I still had the urge to both stay sober and to get drunk. I knew I needed a meeting. I looked up meetings close to me, and I found one that started in the next forty-five minutes at 9 a.m. I went and got some coffee, and I filled up my car with gas to kill some time. Then I went to where the meeting was held to learn that the 9 a.m. meeting was only on Sundays. Google was wrong! Frustrated and desperate, I looked up other meetings, and there was one about twenty minutes away in Oakwood. To Oakwood, I went.

I called my alcoholic friend to see about a meeting in Flowery Branch because I know she goes there for morning meetings on Tuesdays and Thursdays. She answered. I told her about my morning and asked about the meeting she goes to on Thursdays. She said it wasn't her home group, but she goes to a meeting in Oakwood on Thursdays . . . the same one I was on my way to! We talked on the phone while we both drove to the same Oakwood meeting. I was almost there when I got a call from my brother. I put my friend on hold and answered.

He said, "Did you forget to leave something here yesterday?"

I looked in my rearview mirror at the car seats. I told him since I watched the kids yesterday and was going to again tomorrow, I figured he would get his wife's car seats to use for today.

He said, "Well, she's at work, and Blakely needs to get to school."

I then put him on hold and switched back to my friend. "Now get this! I am practically at the meeting, and my brother just called saying he needs the car seats that are in my car to take my niece to school. What do I do now? I need a meeting!"

She talked through various options with me, but it was settled that I needed to get to my brother's house so Blake could get to school. I passed the church where the meeting was to be held and made my way to my bro's. My friend talked with me and said we kind of had a "mini-meeting" together. She shared with me her morning devotion of, "Be still and know that I am God."

Emotionally drained from the morning excitement, wanting to relapse, and fighting to stay sober, I arrived at my brother's. To save time, everyone jumped in the car with me instead of me putting the car seats in his car. So, I drove my brother, my niece, and my nephew to Blakely's preschool. I was starting to reach the point where I felt so tired that all I wanted to do was curl up in a ball in my bed. I told my brother about my chaotic morning.

His response: "I'm glad you didn't do something stupid."

After dropping Blakely at school, I thought of some service work that I did not feel like doing but I knew would be healthy for me and my sobriety. P always says service work or doing for others helps one to get outside of themselves; basically it will get me out of my own head and focus on someone else. My brother agreed to join. My brother, nephew, and I took breakfast to my grandmother (she ended up staying in Georgia and not moving away). My grandmother was very grateful. Afterwards, I dropped my brother and his son off at his house (along with the car seats), and then I made my way home while leaving a lengthy voicemail for my sponsor.

My brother's parting words were, "Don't go and do something stupid."

My brother is not the most emotionally sensitive of guys, but it meant a lot that he acknowledged my struggle and wanted me to stay sober.

I changed out of my fancy work clothes into something comfy. I did a devotion, laid in my bed and listened to a meditation, and prayed. I was exhausted. I had on my sleep mask, and my sweet Buster curled up with me. I kept repeating, "Be still and know that I am God. Be still and know that I am God," over and over and over. Suddenly, I felt this warmth like a light was shining on me. And my eyes were closed and covered by a sleep mask, but I swear it felt like a light was shining right on my face. I felt peace. I felt God. I even opened my eyes and peeked out of my sleep mask to make sure the sun had not come out and shone on me. Nope, I was still in my dimly lit room. It was a breathtaking experience.

I never made it to a meeting, but I used countless tools to help me make it through the day sober. I reached out to another alcoholic and to my sponsor. I was honest with my family about my struggles. I attempted to go to multiple meetings. I rested. I prayed. I meditated. I listened. And, thanks to all of that, God showed me that His plans for me today were not to relapse. I am not sure what the point of His plan was, but I do know that I tried to follow it to the best of my ability instead of following the self-destructive plan I had thought of for myself with relapsing. God gave me the strength to follow through with His plan, not mine. Prayer answered.

~344 days sober

Dry Run

There is a theory on why we have nightmares. Essentially, it is to expose a person to a dangerous situation—one sparking fear, anxiety, etcetera—and it is an opportunity to react to the situation. Thus, when and if you are faced with the situation in real life, you already have prior experience to pull from. You can either act similarly as you did in your dream, or, based on how you responded in your dream, you can modify or act the opposite.

I still do not know God's reason for my fake start date at work last week, but maybe it was to give me a "dry run"—pun intended. I had urges to drink, driving to my new job last week. I had past memories flash in my mind as I drove past the liquor store I used to buy from on lunch breaks at my old job. Last week, I was worn down, but I still chose the *right* action. As my sponsor has lovingly reminded me a million and a half times, I am responsible for taking the *right* action, and God is responsible for the outcome.

Today, driving into work (they have given me a badge and have allowed me into the building, so I think I really am starting today!), I did not have any urges to drink, to relapse . . . nothing. I hardly even remember passing the liquor store on my way in!

Overall, my emotions have been tamer both today and leading up to today. After the obstacles it has taken to start this job, I have already expressed a lot of excitement and anxiety that, by the time I have finally gotten here, to my first day, I'm just *chill*.

Currently, I am sitting here waiting for orientation to start. Of course, I got here early. I am grateful to God and my sponsor for the chips I still hold.

~348 days sober

The Sum

"Success is the sum of small efforts, repeated day in and day out."

—Robert Collier[65]

This quote is from my daily motivation from my sober tracking app, "I Am Sober." It is perfect because, right now, I am sitting in a 6 a.m. meeting in Gainesville, GA. My current shift at my new job is 7 a.m.–2 p.m. I am trying hard to keep my sobriety a priority because I know that if I don't, my sobriety will go down the drain like the wine and vodka I poured down my sink a year ago. It is both a priority and a requirement to attend meetings that I hardly had any anxiety about coming to a meeting I have never been to before with people I have never met before. I thank God for that. I also thank God for the courage to speak up, introduce myself, and share. Why be nervous? I am amongst my brothers and sisters.

This meeting has a sign hanging up, stating, *The Four Absolutes: Honesty, Unselfishness, Love, and Purity.*

~350 days sober

Fear of Economic Insecurity

As stated in the promises of the Alcoholics Anonymous program, "Fear of people and of economic insecurity will leave us."[66] I have written about this before, but this is the topic of the meeting I am in. Fear of economic insecurity. Living day to day with that fear is how I lived for a long time.

While married, we made enough money but we were not smart with it—and that would stress the crap out of me! I was a saver, and he was a spender. When we divorced, I was still living a two-income life on one salary. My savings account became lower and lower. Then my checking account became lower and lower. Then, I went down to part time to focus on my worsening mental and emotional health. Then I quit my job. Then I decided to get sober and could not emotionally handle working night shifts at the restaurant (the shifts that made the most money . . . but also the shifts that served the most alcohol). I was

---

65. http://www.robertcollier.wwwhubs.com/
66. *Alcoholics Anonymous (4th ed.)—"The Big Book"* (2017), p. 84.

slowly building my caseload with my clients at the private practice I was (and still am) working for. Then, I felt God was leading my heart in another direction career-wise. Besides still seeing one client, my income was solely lunch shifts at the restaurant—not enough for a mortgage, insurance, car payments, etcetera. I found a job as an assistant for an accountant, but that was temporary. I craved employment in my chosen field. I searched for employment for four months before finding a job that just started this past week. The bright side of hardly making any money last year was that I got money back after I filed my taxes.

What I think God wanted me to learn last year is that money is not everything. The lack of money has been a motivation to find a job, but it is not the reason for living. They say the root of all evil is money. For a long time, financial insecurities were one cause of my depression, anxiety, and overall misery. But now, even though I have not received my first paycheck yet, I am wealthy. I am spiritually wealthy. I am wealthy with family and friends. I am wealthy with all God has provided me with. I am blessed.

~351 days sober

Joy

My mom coined the phrase, "The dark time," to encapsulate the time frame in which I struggled heavily with my mental illness during high school. Correction: the time frame where my whole family struggled. We did not know what mental illness was outside of ADHD. What was depression outside of situational? Outside of temporary sulking and then having the ability to pull oneself out of it? We didn't know. I bring this up because, during that time, my mom would tell me she did not wish and pray for happiness; rather, she prayed that I would experience joy.

Yesterday, I shared with my sponsor how I have been feeling at the end of the day since I have started my new job. I told her how grateful I am to be working full time again . . . to be speaking clinically again . . . to have a more active role in the mental health field again . . . and how I feel whole.

She responded by saying, "Do you know what you're describing?"

I said, "A pink cloud I'll eventually fall through?"

"No," she said, "It's joy."

Wow.

~352 days sober

The 7 Ts

Take
Time
To
Think
Through
Things
Thoroughly

~360 days sober

Meeting Reflection

Someone shared, "How does relapse start?" and then answered their own question by saying, "When the bed is warm, and I've got a cute puppy snuggling with me."

My gosh. I can completely understand that! Wake up next to Buster and Frankie . . . wake up snuggled in my sheets . . . feel the cool air coming down from the fan. *I think I'll skip the meeting and stay in bed today.* Then it would just be a domino effect from there. Of course, there have been meetings I skip, and I haven't relapsed. But I notice that when I skip a few meetings, it is harder to get back on track and go to a meeting again. So if I were to *stay* off track with my meeting attendance, I can see how that would end in relapse.

~360 days sober

Sharing My New Reality: Part I

Someone shared, "The sooner we disclose to our counterparts, the better it is for remaining sober."

I have a date coming up, and I am unsure how that will go. Do I share my reality and what it's become? My sober life? Living by God's will (or at least trying my best to)? I don't know. I will pray about it.

~361 days sober

Sharing My New Reality: Part II

Date number two happened this morning. Obviously, the first one went well enough to have a second. I told him on the first date that I was living a life of sobriety and was almost a year sober—not many more details than that. I felt comfortable sharing. It was also a way to bring up alcohol and see if he is a big drinker. I definitely wasn't asking, "How much do you drink?" because it is his personal choice to drink. I fear if someone I am with stops drinking because of me, they may grow to resent me. However, I was comforted when he shared that he wasn't a big drinker.

We met at 5:45 this morning at Waffle House. Cute, right? I have the day off of work, but I needed to make my 7 a.m. meeting, and he had to get to work at 7 a.m. I have struggled to make meetings consistently since starting my new job and my shift constantly changing. I told myself, *If I can wake up early for a date, I can get my butt to a meeting!*

~363 days sober

Prayer and Self-Will

This morning's meeting is about self-will. I shared how I became aware that I was praying for my will instead of God's. It was around the time I was working on the 11th step. There was Facebook coverage on a specific pod of Orcas. Apparently, a juvenile Orca had died somehow, and then its grieving mother was swimming around with its child's lifeless body in its mouth. It broke my heart. Day after day, there was a new update with the grieving mother still clasping onto its young. I felt for this mother. I hated that it was suffering such a loss. I found myself praying to God that the mother whale would find the strength to let go of her young and be able to move forward with her grief.

Then I realized, *What the heck do I know?* This could be a regular grieving ritual for Orcas. Or, it could be a special case . . . but it didn't matter! I was praying for what I thought was best for the whale. I was praying for what I thought should happen. Only God knows what should or shouldn't happen. Instead, I prayed that God would be with that grieving whale (technically, Orcas are dolphins) and that His will would be done. Ever since, I check myself and check my words that I am praying for God's will to be done, not mine.

~364 days sober

Meeting Reflection

Someone said . . .
"I don't miss throwing up in bushes, but I miss drinking."
"I don't miss blackouts and forgetting what I did, but I miss drinking."
"The only easy day for me was yesterday."

Yup. I get it.

~364 days sober

1 Year

One year. Holy crap! I made it. All my family that could make it attended my A.A. meeting to see me pick up my 1-year chip—my mom, dad, and brother! My sister-in-law had to stay home with the kids or else I know she would have been there too. My sponsor was there amongst some other friends I have made on this sobriety journey.

I picked up my blue chip today. I shared the story I wrote last year called "Day 60." I shared that even though I had successfully made it through that day 60, I relapsed days later on day 67. I shared how wicked this disease is and how, with all the knowledge I had at the time about how cunning, powerful, and baffling[67] this disease is, I still went back to drinking. But, ultimately, I came back to the rooms. After I shared, I noticed some wet eyes and runny noses. I sat back down in between my mom and brother.

My brother put his arm around me and said, "That was wild," as he maintained his grip on my shoulder. I can still feel the warmth of his hand, the warmth of his love and support.

It is often said in this program, as it is said in Step 3, that this program is about learning to *turn it over*. That, my friends, is nothing that is done easily, nor should it be taken lightly. Turning it over to God has taken courage, vulnerability, faith, trust, failure, strength, weakness, determination, and willpower. My alcoholism placed me in a position that was beyond human aid. Turning it over was my only option left if I wanted to survive.

---

67. *Alcoholics Anonymous (4th ed.)—"The Big Book"* (2017), pp. 58–59.

I used to describe myself as lonely. But now I know that I am never alone because I walk with God daily. I have come to believe that my desire for sobriety can be greater than my compulsion to drink. I had to learn to be OK about losing the power of choice as it pertains to alcohol. But I still have the power to choose God, to choose my sobriety, and to choose my program. The 1st step is in past tense: I "was" powerless, and I continue to remain powerless over alcohol. But with God, I am powerful because He is more powerful than anything on this earth. I used to feel irritable, restless, and discontented[68] daily. Now, I feel such feelings infrequently. I have come to believe that my desire for sobriety can be greater than my compulsion to drink. God has relieved me from my obsession and physical craving for the drink.

In one year, my life has changed drastically. I have experienced torture, sometimes self-inflicted. I have experienced joy. I have experienced many highs and lows. More and more, there are highs. Less and less, there are lows. I am grateful for my life and what it has become. I am sober.

~365 days sober

---

68. *Alcoholics Anonymous (4th ed.)*—*"The Big Book"* (2017), p. xxviii.

Author's Afterword

Since my last entry, my life has continued to grow and evolve. I have been given the gift of what my sponsor has told me is "emotional sobriety" in my second year of sobriety. My thoughts and emotions are even clearer and sharper. During my first year and a half of sobriety, I still missed drinking. I missed the social aspect. Or, I missed just being able to have a glass of wine with dinner. I missed the simple pleasures with alcohol. But, intellectually, I could recognize all that I had gained in my sobriety: an amazing relationship with God; improved relationships with family; more engaged relationships with my niece and nephew; improved finances; a consistent sleeping pattern; healthier mind, body, and soul; the list goes on and on! I knew that I *could not* and *should not* drink again because it would ruin everything. Around two years of sobriety, it truly settled in my mind and my heart that I *would not* trade this sober life for alcohol.

Have you seen in TV or movies where it shows a fast-forward clip of a busy city like Atlanta, New York City, or Tokyo? And the cars are nothing but blurs of tail lights because the cars are moving so quickly? That used to be my brain in active addiction and early recovery. Relentless thoughts. Exhausting, never-ending, relentless thoughts. Have you seen in TV or movies where it shows one car pull up to a four-way stop in the middle of nowhere? Then it shows a tumbleweed blow by in the background to emphasize the emptiness of the location? That's my brain now. One car at a time. Manageable pace. Intentional. It is beautiful, and it is something that I would not trade to have a "simple pleasure" of a glass of wine with dinner.

I now have sponsees! I have others that are trusting me to help them walk this path of sobriety . . . me! When I reflect on my first year of sobriety, I wouldn't be where I am today without God, X, P, Alcoholics Anonymous, and my family.

X played a crucial role in helping me see that I had a problem with alcohol. I had inklings, sure, but she helped me face them. X also helped me face and manage my ongoing mental illness, PTSD, and trauma symptoms that were compounding my alcoholism. I was seeing X twice a week when I was struggling to put mere hours of sobriety time together. Now I have over 2 years of sober time together. Now I am stable. Now my PTSD symptoms have vanished. I only check in with X as needed, sometimes going months and months in between sessions. I encourage you to find your own X to help guide you.

My temporary sponsor played a vital role for me, and I don't know where I'd be without her. Without her, I might not have P. It can be normal to switch sponsors for whatever reason, just as I had a temporary sponsor before finding P. Sometimes a sponsor might get a new job or move, or something changes in their life that makes them less accessible. Or, something might happen where your needs as a sponsee are not being met. It is important, as a sponsee, to recognize what your needs are, to openly discuss them with your sponsor, and to see if it is best to continue with them or if they have someone else in mind who might work better for you. Or maybe you have someone else in mind. All of this is to say, you aren't stuck with anyone. Pray, talk to God. Do what is best for you and your sobriety.

Since finishing this book, I have continued to have P as my sponsor. In the beginning, I called her daily, if not multiple times a day. She was my lifeline. P always told me to not "stay in my head alone." She told me doing so was dangerous. P knew my tendency was to isolate, withdraw, and overthink. She pushed me to call and share my thoughts because my disease and my sickness was wrapped up in my thoughts—as I referenced in the previous pages, in my "stinkin' thinkin'."

I am blessed with a supportive family. I hurt them by being absent. I hurt my brother specifically in a way that I'm not sure will ever be healed. I made amends to all of them, and they have all expressed their support of me. I say I have been blessed with them because I have seen first-hand in the recovery community how it could be very different. I recommend that you stay close to the family that is supportive. Make amends to the ones that you can—to the ones that it won't cause harm. I have witnessed A.A. members come into the A.A. rooms abandoned and alone. I've watched them work the program and rebuild relationships with their families and loved ones. I have seen broken marriages come back to life. I've seen hurt and neglected children move back into their parents' homes. I have witnessed love, forgiveness, and hope in Alcoholics Anonymous.

For anyone reading this book, struggling with addiction: I encourage you to go to a meeting, find a sponsor, and, if you are able, find a therapist. Sobriety is possible. It is often said you have to reach your "rock bottom." Your bottom doesn't have to involve losing your spouse, your job, your home, etcetera. My bottom was losing myself emotionally. I lost my entire self to alcohol. My identity, my soul, my allegiance . . . it was all to alcohol. I didn't know who I was without it. It was killing me. I was dead inside. I felt it wasn't going to be much longer before I was dead on the outside too. I stopped myself from crashing my car when the suicidal urges came that one morning. There was no telling if I was going to stop myself the next time.

Even if you aren't sure that you have a problem, *talk to someone.* As P always says, just don't stay in your head alone.

~823 days sober

Resources

Alcoholics Anonymous (4ᵗʰ ed.)—"The Big Book." 2017. NY: A.A. World Services, Inc.

As Bill Sees It: The A.A. Way of Life. 2001. NY: A.A. World Services, Inc.

Bill P., Todd W., Sara S. 2005. *Drop the Rock: Removing Character Defects (2ⁿᵈ ed.).* Center City, MN: Hazelden Publishing.

Daily Reflections. 2016. NY: A.A. World Services, Inc.

Twelve Steps and Twelve Traditions—"The 12 & 12." 2017. NY: A.A. World Services, Inc.

Johnson, Lynette 2019. *The Girl with the Zebra Leg,* Collierville, TN: Innovo Publishing. Learn how to find encouragement and resiliency through trials. Paperback & eBook. Amazon.com or B&N.com

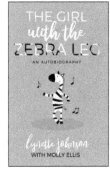

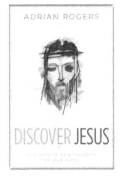

Rogers, Adrian 2020. *Discover Jesus: The Author and Finisher of Our Faith.* Collierville, TN: Innovo Publishing. Learn how to become a new creation and overcome the world. Paperback & eBook. Amazon.com or B&N.com.

CPSIA information can be obtained
at www.ICGtesting.com
Printed in the USA
LVHW051310121220
673922LV00007BA/554

9 781613 145784